CHEAP TRICK

A DAWSON FAMILY NOVEL

EMILY GOODWIN

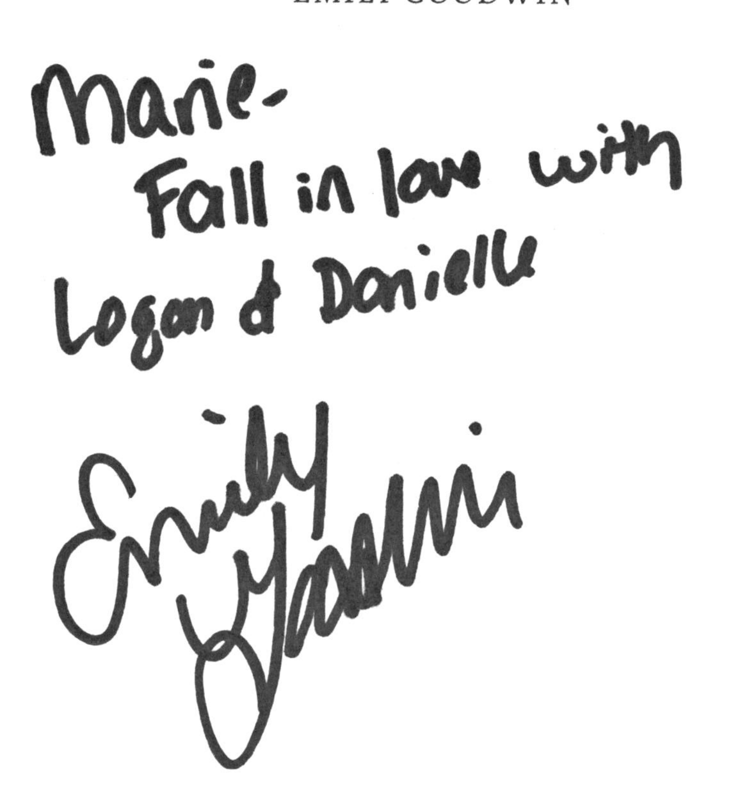

Cheap Trick
A Dawson Family Novel

Cover photography by Braadyn Penrod
Editing by Contagious Edits and My Brother's Editor

Created with Vellum

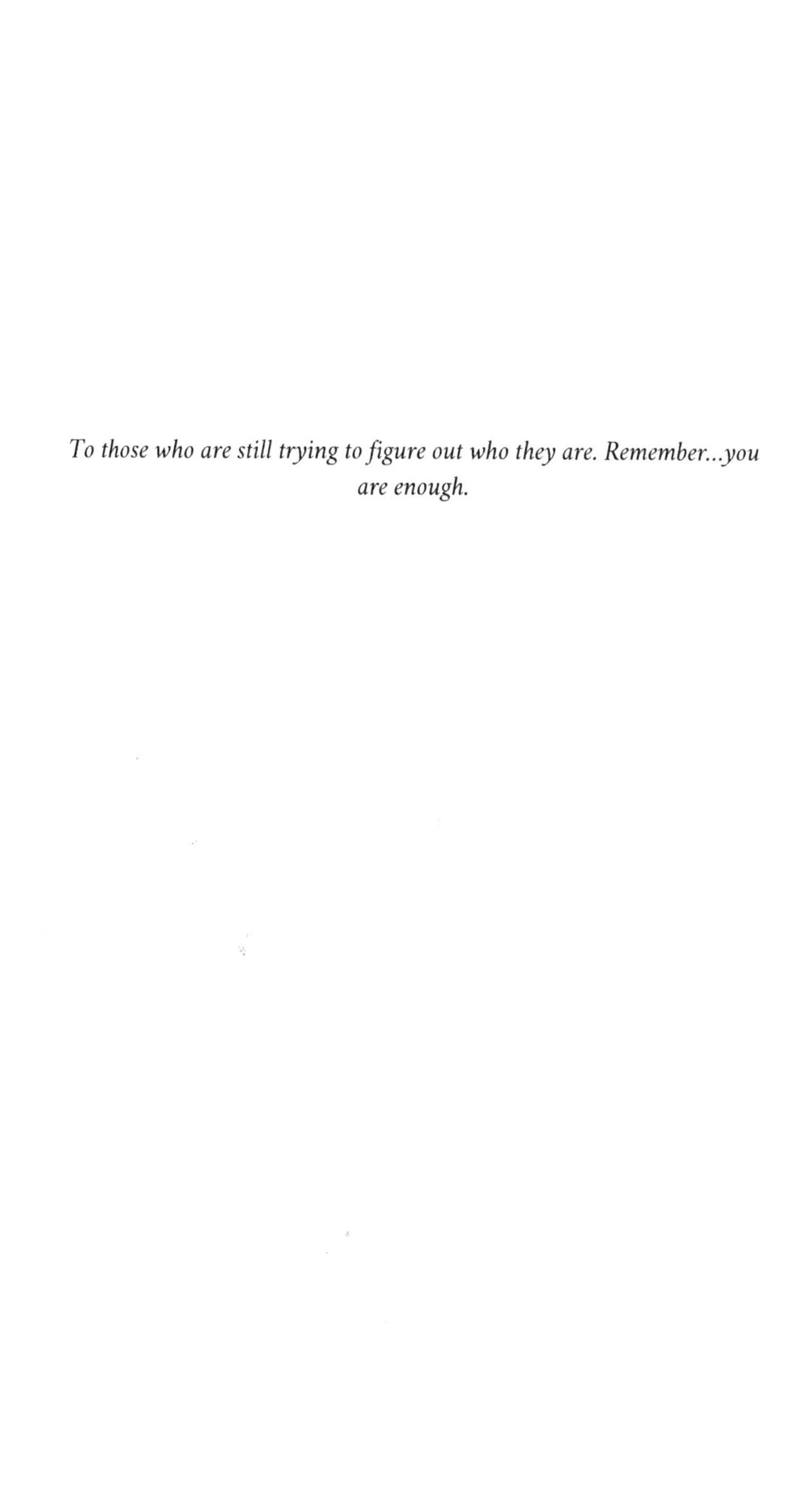

To those who are still trying to figure out who they are. Remember...you are enough.

PROLOGUE

DANIELLE

ONE YEAR AGO...

Someday, I'll stop lying to myself. When I say I'm going to get my life together, I'm going to actually do it.

Someday...just not today.

I pull PJs out of my suitcase and sit on the bed, looking around the room. It's been over ten years since I've been here, and everything is exactly the same, from the pale yellow wallpaper to the faint smell of lavender that fills the house. Gathering up my PJs and toothbrush, I silently move through the hall and into the bathroom, changing and getting ready for bed.

It's been one hell of a day, and I'm exhausted. But of course, as soon as I lie down, I'm wide the fuck awake. After tossing and turning for an hour, I get up and go into the kitchen, finding a bottle of wine in the back of the pantry. I uncork the wine and take it onto the back porch, taking solace in the quiet chorus of crickets.

The screen door slowly creaks open, startling me. "Can't sleep?" Grandpa asks, stepping onto the porch.

I shake my head. "It's probably the jet lag."

Grandpa laughs. "I didn't know you'd get jet lag traveling from Connecticut to Indiana."

I nod. "There's like an hour time difference. It might take me weeks to get used to this."

Grandpa's eyes go to the bottle of wine in my hand. "Are you sure you're okay, kiddo?"

I force a smile, trying hard to hold up the front that I'm A-okay. It's what I always do, but right now, I'm just tired. "Yeah, I am." My fake smile grows wider.

Leaving's always been an option, and it's what I've done over the last few years. When Roger and I broke up, I applied to grad school two states away. When grad school got hard, I took time off to work and build my resume. And when I got let go from my job, I spent three months volunteering in Costa Rica.

And here I am in Indiana.

"Really?" Grandpa's knee cracks as he crosses the porch, sitting on a rocking chair next to me. "Because those who are fine don't sit alone in the dark drinking cheap wine out of a bottle."

I let my eyes fall closed for a few seconds before taking a breath and turning to my grandpa. "I wanted to warn Diana and keep her from being disappointed later in life, but I get the blame for Peter being a Grade-A douchebag and it cost me my job…it feels like I failed. And then when I look back at my life, I see there's been a lot of failure in there."

"How lucky you are that you get to fail. You can only fail if you're living, and that's not something you should ever take for granted."

Tears burn at the corners of my eyes, and I bring the bottle of wine to my lips, taking another drink.

"And you know what else is good about failure?" Grandpa asks. "After each failure, each fall, you get up and you try again. And you might fail again, but you get back up. Each and every time, you *get back up*."

Throat tight, I nod and look out at the farmland. There's a

barn not far from the house, and two of the three horses have their heads hanging out the open Dutch doors. I've always considered myself more or less scrappy and have been able to climb and crawl out of some shitty situations. But once I'm standing on my own two feet again, I'm lost. "I don't know where to go after I get back up."

Grandpa smiles. "Let's start with getting you a decent drink."

"There's a place open around here?"

"Eastwood is a small town, and every small town has at least one good bar. And I mean one. Getaway is open until three of or four AM some nights," he says, waving me back into the house.

"Grandpa!" I exclaim, faking shock. "You stay out until three AM? I thought I was going to be the crazy partier rocking the ship here. You're gonna have me beat."

"I could drink you under the table, kid." He gives me a wink. "Go change and meet me in the truck in five minutes."

"Deal," I say with a laugh. Normally, I'd do my hair and makeup to go to a bar, but tonight I don't give a damn. I throw on jeans, a black top, and red heels. I cave and put on mascara and lip gloss, but I'm still ready in just about five minutes. I comb my hair with my fingers as I walk through the old farmhouse and outside, getting in the passenger side of my grandpa's old pickup truck.

"Lucky for us, the bar isn't far from here," he says and pulls down the driveway.

"Isn't everything ten minutes from anything? The town is small, right?"

"Small in the sense of population, but we have a lot of farmland."

"Yeah. I forgot how peaceful it is out here."

"I still don't understand how your mother could leave all this behind," Grandpa says ruefully. He turns on the radio right after that, flipping through stations. Only country music comes in.

The bar is crowded for a Thursday night. I feel like I'm

walking through a movie set or something with all the pickup trucks parked in a gravel parking lot. Music drifts from the bar, and people sit on tailgates, talking and laughing. I hate that I love it so much.

Grandpa goes right up to the bar, and the bartender knows his name.

"Hey, Fred," he says. "What are you doing here so late?"

"I'm taking my granddaughter out for a night on the town. She just got in from the east coast," Grandpa tells him.

I turn around, taking it all in. This place is pretty damn neat, actually, and is filled with a lot of people my age and not the rednecks and truckers I thought would be here. I'm stereotyping, I know, and I feel bad about it.

"Ellie," Grandpa says, and I don't have the heart to tell him I don't go by that anymore. "This is Logan. He owns the joint."

"Co-owns," someone else says, coming up behind me. I turn, and dammit, my heart skips a beat. Because this man is all sorts of gorgeous. Tall and muscular. Deep hazel eyes. The perfect amount of stubble covers his chiseled jaw. "Right?" He looks at the guy Grandpa is talking to. I take a step to the side so I can see him and do a double-take.

Because that man looks just like the hottie who's behind me. I look back. Holy shit. They're identical twins.

"Hey," the one my grandpa introduced as Logan says. His eyes meet mine and I recognize something in them. A distance, maybe? A longing for the thing that will finally make his empty heart feel full? I only know because I feel the same way. It's a strange moment, one I can't fully explain, and one I'm blaming on the old bottle of cheap wine. But I see something in him, something that differs him from his twin, and I know from that moment on, I'll always be able to tell the two apart. "Welcome to Eastwood. First drink's on the house."

"Thanks," I tell him, feeling a bit of color rush to my cheeks. Grandpa gets two guys at the bar to give up their stools. We sit and he orders me a bourbon on the rocks. I've been a cheap wine drinker my whole adult life. I'm a lightweight when it comes to the hard stuff.

I sip my whiskey faster than I intended and am drunk by the time I finish my drink. Grandpa gets up to throw darts with someone he knows, and I tell him I'm going to stay at the bar, happy to just people watch.

Logan sets another bourbon on the bar top, switching it out for my empty glass. "Second one's on the house too. You look like you've had a night."

I cock an eyebrow, not sure if I should take it as an insult or not. "What gave that away? It couldn't possibly be the fact that I came to a bar at one AM on a Thursday with my grandpa."

Logan laughs and my God that man is gorgeous. I slide the whiskey over and take a sip, trying to look seductive but end up clipping the glass against my teeth and sloshing it down my face.

"Are you going to be in town long?" Logan asks, grabbing empty glasses from the bar.

"I don't know," I reply after I take another drink. Really, I have nowhere else to go. Eastwood was a last resort, and I'm tired of running from my problems. They tend to find me no matter where I go. But I have no reason to stay. Logan gets busy and I turn around, drink in hand, and notice a *now hiring* sign hanging in the window by the door.

I bite the inside of my cheek, mind going a million miles an hour. Before I have a chance to actually think this through, I spin back around in my barstool and set my drink down.

"Hey," I say, getting Logan's attention. "You're hiring?"

He nods. "You interested?"

I smile. "Yeah. I am."

CHAPTER 1

LOGAN

"That is disgusting, sis," I tell Quinn, shaking my head as I watch her pull maraschino cherries out of a glass of vodka with a spoon. "You know I can make you a real drink, right?"

She pops one in her mouth and nods. "I do, but I kinda like this. Actually, go ahead and make me one. You still owe me for filing your taxes."

"You want another drink on top of that?" Dean raises his eyebrows, playing the part of concerned older brother too well. "Haven't you had enough?"

"Fuck, you're so lame," Owen quips, clapping Dean on the back. "Drink as much as you want, Quinn. On the house."

"Don't tempt me," Quinn laughs, getting another cherry out of her cup. "I have a very small window to enjoy alcohol before Archer knocks me up again. Like tonight."

Dean wrinkles his nose, put off as always by the thought of his childhood friend marrying—and knocking up—our sister. "That's even more disgusting than the vodka-cherries."

Quinn laughs, enjoying poking at Dean. I go back around the bar, making drinks for a few customers before bringing Quinn a

Jack and Coke, trading it for the glass of cherries. It's a weekday night, but the bar is busy, as it always is. I go back and forth between filling drink orders, cleaning up spilled booze, hassling Owen to do his fucking job, and talking with Quinn and Dean, who are waiting for Archer to get off work to join them.

A storm is blowing in, and the power flickers. We have a generator, but it's still a pain in the ass to deal with. Though storms always seem good for business. People still come in despite the weather, but those who are already here tend to order an extra drink and wait out the rain.

I'm wiping down the bar top when a clap of thunder booms overhead, rattling the windows. I look up at that exact moment, and the door to the bar swings open. Danielle walks in, and a feeling I try to ignore bubble in my stomach. Her long, brunette hair is down today, hanging in waves around her face. The white t-tank top she has on is speckled with raindrops. Immediately, my mind goes to what she'd look like if her shirt were completely drenched.

She looks through the crowd, meets my eye, and smiles as she makes her way over. The whole world stops when she's around, and looking at her now isn't much different than looking at her for the first time. Her sea-green eyes shine no matter how dim it is in the room. The energy around her is magnetic, drawing you in even if you try to resist.

And trust me, I've resisted.

I push all feelings aside, trying to convince myself Danielle is just one of the guys, and smile back.

"You must really miss me," I quip, raising my eyebrows as Danielle comes up to the bar. "I mean, to come in on your day off just to see me."

Danielle snags a seat at the bar and rolls her eyes. "Busted. Those secret photos I have of you weren't doing the job. My plan was to 'accidentally' leave my phone out and hope you'd take the hint I need a dick pic or two."

I laugh as I reach under the counter for a glass. "I'm sure I can get you at least a dozen dick pics. Can't promise it'll be of mine. You can't handle all that."

Laughing, Danielle makes a show of running her eyes up and down me. It's meant in fun, but her smile starts to fade and a flush comes to her cheeks. Blinking rapidly, she looks away, reaching up for a strand of her hair to twist around her fingers.

"What are you doing here?" I pour whiskey into her glass and slide it over.

She brings the glass to her lips and takes a big sip. "My grandpa has a *lady friend* over." She shudders. "And Adele doesn't like to drive in the rain so she's staying the night." She takes another sip of whiskey and slowly shakes her head. "I didn't want to risk overhearing anything." She sets the glass down, looking up at me with wide eyes. "And it also made me realize that even dear old gramps has a better love life than I do."

I hate that I like hearing that. I don't want her to have a love life with anyone who's not me. I laugh again and set the bottle of whiskey on the counter in front of her.

"You need this tonight. Drown your sorrows. And Quinn is here. Maybe you can take one of her cats and slowly start living out your fate as a crazy cat lady."

"Thanks, Dawson," she spits and takes the whiskey. Snickering, I step to the side, taking a drink order from one of our regulars. I give Mr. Fenton his beer and lean on the counter in front of Danielle again.

"Your sister would never give up one of her cats." She finishes her whiskey and pours a little more in her glass.

"Never hurts to ask."

Danielle cocks an eyebrow. "I'd rather keep my head."

I laugh again and see Archer walk through the door of the bar. "Ask him first. He'll gladly give you two or three."

Danielle turns and sees Archer. She shakes her head and turns back around. "He's so whipped. He'd come home with another two or three if Quinn really wanted them."

"Sadly, I think you're right."

Archer looks around the bar for Quinn and Dean but sees us first. Danielle waves and he comes over, saying hi before going over to join the others. Danielle pours another splash of whiskey in her glass and gives the bottle back to me, and then goes over and sits by Quinn as well.

I'm nonstop busy for the next half-hour or so, and for the life of me can't find Owen. He's probably in the office hooking up with someone, making me not even want to go looking. Danielle's not the only one lacking in their love life.

Owen has set me up on more dates than I can count over the last few months. We even went out with another set of identical twins. I ended the night early and Owen took them both home. He still won't let me live that down.

But they don't measure up.

"You just gonna stand there with your dick in your hand?" Owen comes up behind me.

I turn, cocking an eyebrow. "What the fuck are you talking about?"

"It's basically what you're doing." Owen runs a hand through his hair, trying to smooth it out. He was hooking up, that fucker. "If she wasn't so damn good at telling us apart, I'd make a move, have her think it was you, and force your hand."

I shake my head, opening my mouth to say some smartass comment back when Danielle stands and waves us over.

"It's not too late to go trade clothes," Owen tries.

"You smell like a cheap hooker. Even Scarlet could tell us apart tonight."

Owen chuckles and attempts to fix his hair again. We both have a cowlick on the back of our heads, making our hair naturally messy. It bothered me when I was younger, but now I know how to make the rugged look work for me. Owen grabs a beer and pops off the top.

"You're drinking away your paycheck again."

Owen ignores me and goes over to the table, grabbing a chair from another and sliding it over.

"What, no more whiskey?" Danielle holds up her empty glass.

I give her a look. "You work here."

"Not tonight," she reminds me with a laugh.

I pull up another chair and crowd around the table.

"Owen will agree with me," Quinn says, green eyes wide.

"Probably," Owen says with a shrug. "What am I agreeing to this time?"

"Service cats."

"Service cats?" Owen takes a drink of beer.

Quinn nods enthusiastically. "Service cats are the thing of the future."

Archer gives Quinn a look. "They'd just knock shit over and make you trip. On purpose. And then feast on your flesh."

Quinn narrows her eyes and Archer shakes his head, laughing.

"Fine. Cats are majestic creatures," he says in a level tone. "I'm so lucky we have six of them."

"Don't act like you don't like them," Quinn quips. "I'm not the one who ordered that six-foot cat tree off Amazon last night."

"It looks like a palm tree. They're going to love it."

Danielle nudges my leg under the table. "Told you it'd be a death sentence asking for one of them," she whispers, and I laugh.

Thunder booms outside and the power flickers. Someone orders a round of shots, making Owen and I get up and back to work. About an hour later, Quinn, Archer, and Dean leave. Danielle stays and helps close down the bar. She's had a few more drinks and is more than a little tipsy when it comes time to leave.

"Want me to take you home?" I ask her, sticking the register drawer in the safe.

"And risk hearing two old people…" She smashes her hands together. "You know."

"The elderly need love too. Miss *Ladyfriend* Adele will take her teeth out and everything." I wiggle my eyebrows.

"Stop."

"Your gramps is a good-looking guy. I've seen the way those church ladies look at him. And didn't you say he's been volunteering more at the church? I bet that's code for all the pus—"

"Seriously stop!" She laughs and throws a damp bar rag at me and almost loses her footing.

"You're drunk."

"The floor is slippery." She pushes herself up and crosses her arms, holding my gaze. It's something we do quite often, and she's always the first one to lose the little staring contest and start laughing.

I lock up the office and grab my keys. Owen has been wiping the same table for the last few minutes, doing a shitty job trying not to get caught watching us.

"So…do you want me to take you to a friend's house?" I ask, though the few people Danielle hangs out with are Quinn, Scarlet, and her cousin Rebecca, who has four kids and teaches first grade at the local elementary school. I can't imagine she'd be very happy to come unlock the front door right now. "Or do you want to come back to my place?"

This could play out a million ways, but I'm only interested in it ending in one.

"You wouldn't mind me crashing on the couch?"

"You can have my bed and I'll take the couch. I'm pretty beat so I'll pass out as soon as I lie down," I say, hating myself as the words leave my mouth.

Danielle wrinkles her nose, and I have no fucking clue how someone can look that damn adorable and sexy as fuck at the same time. Out of the corner of my eye, I see Owen shaking his head.

"That'd be great then." Danielle pushes off the wall, teetering on her heels a bit when she walks. "I'm going to use the bathroom first."

"Seriously?" Owen says once Danielle is out of earshot. "You're going to pass out as soon as you're on the couch? She's drunk. Now's your chance to make a move. If she rejects you, there's a good chance she won't remember it in the morning."

"I'm not making a move when she's drunk," I deadpan.

"Right. Because you're never going to make a move at all."

"Shut up," I tell my twin, giving him a warning glare. We push each other's buttons like no one else can, perks to being an identical twin, and no one else is allowed to mess with us the way we mess with each other. But even Owen knows there's a line to cross and the heckling over Danielle is inching toward it.

I've had feelings for Danielle since the moment I met her. Sometimes I think the feelings are mutual, but Danielle's made it clear she has no intentions of settling down in Eastwood. Making a move might complicate things, and I don't want to risk what we have.

I'd rather have her in my life as a friend than not at all.

CHAPTER 2

DANIELLE

"Why did I think tequila shots were a good idea?" I rub my forehead, blinking my eyes open to watch the farmland pass us by. Everything is dark, and then a raccoon's eyes reflect in the headlights. It probably won't be long until we see a deer as well. I've learned to drive well below the speed limit on some of these country roads at night. You never know what kind of wildlife will run out in front of you.

Logan laughs softly and reaches into the backseat of his car, pulling a water bottle out of an open case and handing it to me.

"Thanks," I say and go to take it from him. My fingers brush over his, and I'm almost startled by how soft and warm his skin feels against mine. I wonder if the rest of him is just as—nope. I can't go there.

First of all, he's my boss.

And second, what's the point of starting a relationship when I'm not staying here forever? I'm a bit ride-or-die when it comes to dating. I either want casual, first-name-only-basis or we're-in-it-for-the-long-haul kind of deal. Logan has long-haul potential, but I'm kind of a basket case, and he's, well...Logan.

Handsome. Polite. A bit broody and moody, which really just

adds to his charm. His t-shirts are just tight enough to show off his muscles. And that's not to mention his strong jawline that's always covered in the perfect amount of stubble.

Family is important to him, and he's probably one of the most loyal people I know. He loves dogs and likes to read and—shit. I'm doing it again. I twist the cap off the water bottle and chug half of it, feeling much better once the water hits my stomach.

Logan's place isn't far from the bar. I know because I've been there before. Just never at night like this. With the intention of falling asleep there.

Which isn't a big deal. We're friends. And friends let friends crash at their place when they need to. I steal another glance at Logan, getting the most unwelcome feeling of fluttering in my chest. A passing car's headlights illuminate his handsome face and I need to look away.

"Did we forget Owen at the bar?"

"He went home with some girl he met tonight. She was waiting for him to get off work."

I shake my head, laughing. "Hasn't he slept with most of Eastwood by now?"

"He has. I better warn your grandpa Owen's moving into a new age bracket. He should lock things down with Adele to keep Owen from making a move."

"You're such a dick," I laugh, playfully nudging Logan's arm. His skin is warm like I imagined, and my fingers linger just a little too long. Swallowing hard, I shift in my seat and take another drink of water.

Logan messes with the radio and we drive the rest of the short way to his place listening to music and not talking. Yellow light spills from the porch and into the lawn. Logan and Owen live together in a cookie-cutter house in a newer subdivision on the outskirts of Eastwood. The house looks like it was lifted from a middle-aged housewife's Pinterest board, and is the last house I'd expect two eligible bachelors to live in.

It took me by surprise the first time I pulled up to it and was even more shocked when I went inside and saw the professional decorating. Turns out, this neighborhood was developed and built by Mr. Dawson's contracting company. The house Logan and Owen live in now was a model home for a few years, hence the perfect design.

I wobble my way through the garage and into the house.

"Did your mom send you any leftovers?" I ask, balancing on one foot at a time to get my heels off, tossing them to the side of the door.

"Oh of course," Logan says, striding through the kitchen, following the pathetic whimpers of his dog. "But we ate them."

"Dang it. Your mom is a good cook."

"We're having lunch over there tomorrow. Come with." The sound of a metal crate opening echoes through the otherwise quiet house. A five-month-old German Shepherd comes running out, jumping up at Logan, wagging his tail so hard he almost falls over.

"Down," Logan tells him, holding out his hand. It's cute, really, watching him try to be firm with the dog. He always ends up caving, like he is right now as he sits on the floor and lets the dog get up in his face.

"His training seems to be going well," I sass, crossing my arms. "Glad you're really sticking with being firm."

"How can you say no to this face?" Logan pushes the dog's ears back and then scratches Dexter's chest, making his back leg go all crazy.

"Dexter!" I call, sinking down to my knees. Dexter, realizing for the first time that I'm here, comes barreling over. He knocks me back and I fall to the ground, laughing as the lanky pup licks my face.

"Come on," Logan calls. "Go outside."

Dexter bounds away, getting excited when he sees Logan holding his leash. I push myself up, going over to the sink to get something to drink since I somehow forgot about the water bottle in the two seconds it took for me to unbuckle and get out of the car. I fill a glass with water and set it on the counter. The kitchen is relatively clean today. Logan, overall, is a neat person. Living with Owen is like living with an adult-sized toddler leaving messes in every room. It's funny, really, how they look so alike but have such different personalities.

I go into the living room, find the TV remote on the coffee table, and sink onto the couch. I have every intention of turning on a scary movie and making Logan watch it with me. But then I close my eyes, just for a second. The next thing I know, Dexter is on the couch next to me, wagging his tail and licking my face.

"Lightweight." I feel the couch sink down as Logan sits down at my other side.

"Hey," I grumble, slitting my eyes open. "I actually had like three drinks and a shot tonight. That's a lot."

"It is. I'll change that lightweight to a lush then."

"Asshole." I try to throw a pillow at him but just end up smacking him in the face. I push myself up and laugh. "I'm sorry. I didn't mean to."

"Now you've done it." Logan grabs another pillow and chucks it at me. Dexter gets way too excited and pounces on Logan, with one of his large paws landing right between his legs. Logan doubles over in pain, and I laugh even harder.

"Who's the asshole now?" he chokes out.

"Don't call Dexter-Wexter an asshole," I gasp in fake shock and slip my fingers under Dexter's collar, gently pulling him back and off the couch. I get up to grab the pillow I threw and trip when Dexter tries to do a flying leap back onto the couch.

I don't know how he moves so fast, but I'm grateful he did. Because I'm still too drunk to have a good reaction time, and I'm about ready to fall backward onto the glass coffee table.

Logan's arms fold around my waist at the last second. He pulls me to his chest and straightens up. I have one hand on his chest and the other is gripping his bicep. Which is strong. Firm. Warm, just like the rest of him.

A second passes, and we're still standing there like this. I splay my fingers over his chest and turn my head up, looking into his brown eyes. Inhaling deep, my breasts crush against his body. His hand that's on the small of my back inches lower and his fingertips press into my waist.

Heat flashes through me, unlike anything I've felt around him before. I've worked hard to keep these kinds of reactions from happening, but my whiskey-soaked mind has lost all its will right now.

"You okay?" he asks, though by now it's obvious I am.

"Yeah. Lost my balance."

"No shit."

I purse my lips and go to shove him away. Dexter is on the floor behind him now, and Logan trips over the dog and falls back onto the couch, taking me down with him. That same heat ripples through me again, making my skin break out in goosebumps. My heart lurches and is beating so fast I'm sure Logan can hear it.

I should push him away.

Run and hide.

I definitely shouldn't be inching closer, taking note of the way his cologne smells, or the fact that his shirt is pulled up a bit, exposing a few inches of his abdomen.

I shouldn't want more.

Our eyes meet and I part my lips, feeling my heart beating faster and faster in my chest. I know one kiss is all it will take to change things between us, and the thought terrifies me.

My life has been one mistake after another, and each seems to try its damnedest to outdo the last. I love what we have between us. Logan is my best friend. I don't want to mess that up.

But Lord have mercy on me right now. His heart is hammering along with mine, and he looks at me with an intensity I've never seen before. One that heats me from the inside out, melting the panties right off me. My face is moving slowly toward his, eyes zeroed in on his perfect lips. He closes his eyes, long lashes coming together, and inhales, pushing his chest up against mine.

And then Dexter jumps up, barking, startling us both. He runs through the living room and into the kitchen, disappearing into the small mud room to greet whoever just came in the house.

Logan's brows furrow, and I get off of him, too drunk to think logically right now. Whiskey and tequila swirl around in my head, though it's nothing but a small buzz compared to the way Logan just made me feel. He springs to his feet and rushes through the house, and it's only then I remember Owen isn't supposed to be home tonight.

I don't remember locking the door behind us. Eastwood is a slow-moving, peaceful town, but it's not a crime-free paradise. People break in, and there's been a rash of burglaries lately. So far, all have happened to empty houses, but maybe they didn't know we were home.

Suddenly, I'm scared, and I look around the room for a weapon.

"What the fuck are you doing?" Logan asks, but he seems annoyed, not terrified for our lives.

"Miranda's sister brought some friends over. We needed a place a little more private."

I let out a breath. It's Owen. I sink back onto the couch, head spinning. I cup my face in my hands. What the hell was I thinking?

But also…why not?

No. Nope. No way José. I thought with my heart instead of my head my whole life and look where it got me. I've spent the last year making logical choices, and I've never been happier. Hearts are wild things needed to be confined to cages. They can't be trusted.

"What, did I interrupt something?" Owen moves into the kitchen and immediately goes for the fridge. Most of the main floor is an open concept, and the kitchen, breakfast nook, and living room are all one big area. A pretty girl with short black hair follows along behind him, nervously looking at Dexter. The dog is big for a puppy, but he's still in that *I love everyone* phase and hasn't gotten too protective yet.

I close my eyes, feeling the pull of the alcohol making me tired. I let it lull me to sleep, passing out right there on the couch, dreaming of something other than the feelings that are taking me over right now. Though there's just as much of a risk of dreaming about Logan and how good we could be together.

CHAPTER 3

DANIELLE

"I could get used to this view." Scarlet lowers her sunglasses and winks at Weston, Logan's oldest brother and Scarlet's husband.

"They do look good," I agree, stretching my legs out in front of me. We're lying out by the pool at Logan's parents' house, watching all the Dawson brothers help put in a new patio. Sweat drips down Logan's chest, glistening in the sun. I grab my lemonade and take a big sip. I almost kissed Logan last night and watching him move heavy cement pavers is doing bad things to my head.

And even worse things to my body.

It's a hot summer day, but the heat coming off of Logan is no comparison to the noon sun in the middle of June.

"I'm related to them all," Quinn says, shaking her head. "Now I know how Dean feels when Archer and I joke about hooking up."

"Oh, honey." Scarlet pushes her sunglasses back up onto her nose. "You do not joke."

Quinn flushes a bit but laughs. "It is fun to watch Dean recoil in disgust." A cry comes through the baby monitor that's sitting on the side table next to Quinn. She takes another drink of her lemonade and gets up with a sigh. "That was a short nap."

"Want me to get her?" Scarlet asks.

"Thanks, but it's okay. Keep getting that beautiful golden glow one minute in the sun gives you." Quinn makes a face and shakes her head. "It's so unfair."

Scarlet wiggles her hips and laughs. "I've always tanned easily. Which is a good thing. Lying out in a bikini in the front lawn of my Southside apartment was always risky." She shudders and starts to get up. "I should check on Jackson, though. He's watched at least one episode of PAW Patrol now, and it's time to get his little butt back out in the sunshine."

They go inside, leaving me alone to watch Logan, Owen, Dean, and Weston work on the patio. I spend a few minutes admiring them all before I get up as well. I'm hot just sitting here in the sun tanning, let alone doing physical labor. There's always cold beer in the fridge at the Dawson's, and the guys could really use one right now.

Mrs. Dawson and Dean's wife, Kara, are in the kitchen, getting lunch ready for us all. Mrs. Dawson looks up from the stove when I come in, pulling my swimsuit cover-up over my head.

"That smells amazing," I tell her, eyes going to the stove. Then I notice a dish on a tray next to the oven. "Are those pin-wheels?"

"Thanks, and they are!" Mrs. Dawson turns down the burner and steps away from the stove. There's a large island behind her, custom built to fit all seven of the Dawsons around it.

"I volunteered to make them for the church luncheon this Sunday. I have no idea what's in them."

Mrs. Dawson smiles. "I'll give you my recipe as long as you promise not to share it with Karen McAllister."

I laugh. "Deal. And thank you."

"I didn't know you were so involved in the church."

"I'm not really," I say carefully. I don't regularly attend church but went last week with Grandpa after he pestered me to join him over and over. And the only reason I volunteered to do anything with this stupid luncheon was in hopes that Natalie Briggs would like me more. Which sounds so stupid now that I'm thinking about it.

I guess I do want to fit in here…more than I'm willing to admit to myself.

"Well, it'll be nice to see you there. Maybe you can convince a certain son of mine to come with you." She raises her eyebrows, and I'm suddenly really interested in a hangnail I have on my pinky finger.

"So, it's a hot day out there. I was going to get something for the boys to drink."

"Good thinking." Mrs. Dawson beams, and I go to the fridge, pulling out four bottles of beer and taking them back outside. Shirtless and sweaty, Logan and Owen look exactly the same. They carry themselves differently, and I don't think they even notice it. It's the biggest thing that gives them away, even when they try to fool me. Plus, Owen has a small scar on his forehead that Logan doesn't have. If you didn't know to look for it, you wouldn't see it at all.

"Anyone thirsty?" I ask, holding up the bottles of beer. Owen turns to Logan, no doubt about to make a smartass comment, but Logan elbows him hard in the ribs before he gets a chance to get a word out.

Logan takes his beer and motions for me to join him by the side of the pool. I grab my lemonade and stick my feet in. Logan takes a few gulps of his beer, hands it to me, and dives into the pool. I close my eyes and look away, trying to quell the longing in my heart.

"That's much better." He swims to the side of the pool and reaches for his beer. I extend my arm and hand him his beer. He chugs the rest, sets the empty bottle on the side of the pool, and goes underwater again. I lean back, thankful for the hot summer day. No one will question why I'm fanning myself right now.

Swallowing hard, I shut my eyes and think about the pinwheels I need to make for church this coming Sunday.

"Uncle Logan!" a little voice shouts. I open my eyes and sit up, watching Jackson run at full speed toward the pool. Scarlet is right behind him, reaching for his hand. He's faster, and Jackson jumps into the pool. Logan swims forward and grabs him.

"I can swim now," Jackson retorts, pushing Logan away. Logan laughs and lets his nephew go but stays close by just in case. I finish my lemonade and lie back, getting splashed by Jackson and Logan only a minute later. I jerk up, narrowing my eyes and pursing my lips.

"It's on," I warn them and dive in.

~

I TYPE A REPLY ONLY TO DELETE IT. BITING MY LIP, I SHIFT MY EYES from my computer to Orange Cat, a cleverly named orange tabby, I know. He's one of the three barn cats Grandpa has let inside. We also have Black Cat, who is—you guessed it—black. And Tabby, a grey tabby cat. Creativity is obviously not Grandpa's strong point.

Nearly half an hour has passed and I still haven't replied to my sister's email. I don't know what to say. My heart skips a beat in my chest butterflies swarm in my stomach. Closing my eyes, I flop back on my bed, mulling everything over.

I left home—after only being back for a few months—because of the way things went down. My sister's fiancé made a move on me. And I got blamed for it. I'd had too much to drink that night. My dress was too tight. Too short. I showed too much cleavage.

It was all my fault. I couldn't stay there and watch things unfold. Only a few days after I confronted Peter about the shit he pulled, he proposed to my sister. And my lack of support further proved my "jealousy."

I've hardly spoken to my mother, father, or sister since I've come to stay with Grandpa in Eastwood, and I can only imagine what they'd say about the life I've made for myself here. They'd probably be horrified to find out I haven't stepped foot inside a country club or a five-star restaurant—and have no intention to do so. I prefer the slow, hot summer days in rural Indiana, where I get to sit on the front porch with a—gasp—bottle of three-dollar wine in my hand as I watch tractors and horse trailers pulled by big pickup trucks going up and down the road all day.

I've gained a few pounds since I've moved here. Cut my own hair a time or two. And I really like going to the farmer's market every Tuesday morning. This is far from the life I imagined I'd have, but that life was laid out before me with little choice of my own.

Get into a prestigious college? Check. I was a legacy and my father played golf with the Dean of Admissions. I graduated with a business degree and decent grades. Phase one of my life was complete. Now I needed to land an aristocrat asshole of a boyfriend to eventually settle down with and spend our summers in the Hamptons. Roger was tolerable at first, but that ended quickly. I went to Canada before I told my parents we ended things.

I close my eyes and let out a breath. My whole life has been mapped out with the road paved in front of me. I don't know what it's like to stray from the path and figure out who I am. It's a strange and harrowing feeling to have this emptiness inside me, longing to meet the person I'm meant to be.

It's almost as if I miss myself, which doesn't make sense at all, I know.

But what I do know is for each time I've fallen, I've gotten back up, just like Grandpa told me to do. Only, once I'm on my feet I'm left teetering, ready to fall with the next gust of wind. He told me I need to find something to hold onto, something to ground myself, and then put down roots.

I don't know how to do that.

"Fuck you," I say to my computer.

"Are you chatting with an online boyfriend?" Grandpa says, walking past my open bedroom door.

"Hah." I push myself up and raise one eyebrow. "If only." I look back at the computer and shake my head. "It's just another job rejection." The lie leaves my lips before I have a chance to really think about it. All I know is I don't want to bring up Diana's wedding yet. Grandpa has been at odds with my mother since the day she ran off and married my father, who put Roger's assholeness to shame.

Though I'm sure I really do have a rejection email in my inbox somewhere. I'm either overqualified by having a degree and a little bit of grad school under my belt, or I'm lacking experience since I only have a degree and a bit of grad school under my belt. It's an infuriating process that makes me want to give up looking for a job entirely.

"You already have a job."

I raise an eyebrow. "I don't want to bartend the rest of my life."

Grandpa leans against the doorframe. "Why not?"

I open my mouth but can't come up with a legitimate reason right now. "I, uh, I'd like better hours. I work late a lot."

"But you're a night owl, just like me."

"True. I don't know." Shaking my head, I open my computer again. "I guess I just thought I'd be doing something more fulfilling in my life by now. I'm almost thirty and, not that I don't love living here, it's just that, well, I'm living here."

Grandpa gives me a wink. "Feel free to move your shit to the barn then."

I laugh and look back at the computer, heart lurching when I see Diana's email glowing on the screen before me.

"What's really bothering you, Ellie?"

Dammit. Why is he so perceptive? "Diana," I start and let out a breath. "She's getting married this summer and wants to know if we're coming to the wedding since I never responded to her invitation." I shake my head. "I can't believe she's marrying that guy... after everything he did, how can she want to marry him?"

Grandpa lets out a deep sigh. "Some people...some people are as blind as they want to be."

"What do you mean?"

"I mean, they know the truth is right there in front of them, they just choose not to see it."

"Wouldn't that be nice?" I run a hand through my long hair. "I'd give anything to have tunnel vision every now and then."

"You take after me. We're not built for tunnel vision. We see everything, and sometimes seeing everything makes you feel it all too. You may not see how much of a blessing that is now, but someday you will."

The knot in my chest loosens. "Maybe that's why...never mind. It's silly."

"You thought it and almost spoke it. Can't be that silly." Grandpa raises his silver eyebrows. I purse my lips and hold his gaze, looking away only a few seconds later.

"Fine. Maybe seeing everything, feeling everything, is what's distracting me from figuring out who I'm supposed to be. It's like no matter how hard I try to find my place in the world, I just can't. I get one foot up on the ladder only to slip and fall."

"Stop trying," Grandpa says like it's simple. "You are exactly who you're supposed to be."

I force a smile and nod, then motion to the computer. "I don't know how to respond. She wants me to be a bridesmaid."

"Do you want to go?"

It's a simple question, yet it has a weight to it. Saying I don't want to go to my only sister's wedding makes me feel like a terrible person. Diana might value her socialite status more than anything else, but that doesn't mean I don't love my sister and wish her well.

Because I do.

Which is why this is so fucking hard.

Peter is bottom-of-the-barrel scum, hailing from a pedigree-rich family. He's the second son in the Abbington line, but that doesn't mean he won't get his fair share of the family cut. He's a shoo-in to fill someone's position in his father's company and can get Diana into any country club on the east coast just by dropping his last name.

"I want to go to her wedding," I finally admit. "Because I'll regret it if I don't. Besides, if I don't, how will I compare her first wedding to her second? Or third?"

Grandpa laughs. "That's the spirit, kid." He pushes off the wall and heads down to the first level of the house. Each stair creaks under his feet, and the screen door going out to the front porch groans and then snaps shut. Grandpa refuses to fly, so he won't be going to Diana's expensive Maui wedding.

I look at the email from my sister again and take a deep breath as I type.

Hey, Diana,

The wedding is coming up soon and Hawaii is the perfect place to tie the knot! It's so exciting :-) I'd be honored to be in your wedding party, and I'm thrilled you even asked!

"Grow some balls," I mutter to myself and delete everything. I squeeze my eyes shut and start again.

Hey, Diana,

I hope all is going well between you and Peter, and I'd love to be part of your big day. You're my sister, and I will always love you and support you no matter what.

Take care,

Danielle

My words still sound contrived, but I hit send anyway and then quickly close my laptop before I have a chance to regret replying to the email. I really do wish her well. In a perfect world, Peter snapped out of his man-whoring, asshole ways.

But we don't live in a perfect world. We live in the real world, and the real world—more often than not—dishes out its fair share of hard times.

CHAPTER 4

DANIELLE

My phone sounds with an email notification. Normally, hearing that little *ding* never bothers me. But right now, I happen to be waiting on two important emails. I get poor service in the farmhouse, and it's not until I went outside on my way to the barn that my email updated.

I dig my phone out of my back pocket and stop outside the corral fence. All three horses are up here near the barn this evening, waiting to be fed their grain. Sundance plods over, sticking his head over the fence. I reach up, not looking as I run my hand over his soft muzzle.

There's a glare from the sinking sun, and I turn, using the horse for shade so I can read my sister's response.

That's great! I need your measurements so I can have the dress altered for you, and I need the final count to give to the caterers. You're single, right? Only serious plus-ones are invited since this venue is rather exclusive. You'll share a room with another single lady. Looking forward to seeing you.

-D

"I'm sure you are," I grumble, shaking my head. "You're lucky you're a horse," I tell Sundance and pat the side of his face. He cranes his neck, trying to sniff my pockets. "There's nothing in there today, buddy." I laugh as he pushes me, wanting to check the back pockets as well. "I'll go inside and get you a handful of Lucky Charms."

I reread Diana's email again, probably taking things way more personally than I should. I'm quite good at doing that. But it also makes me realize that one of her other bridesmaids must have dropped out at the last minute and that's the real reason she asked me to be a part of her wedding. Why else would she already have a dress?

My phone vibrates with a text right as I grab the cereal box from the cabinet. For a split second, I think it's Diana, but it's Rebecca, saying she's looking forward to hanging out tonight. Right. That's tonight. I didn't forget. I just, uh, fine. I forgot.

Speaking of getting my life together…

I go back upstairs, change into a checkered dress and throw my long hair up into a messy ponytail. I give each horse a handful of the sugary cereal and get in my car, driving into town to Rebecca's house.

"Hey!" she exclaims as she throws back the door, holding up a bottle of wine. Her Yorkie yips at her feet. "Aaron is working late tonight and the kids are at my in-laws. I hope you're ready to party!" She steps aside, letting me in the house. "And by party I mean be gone by ten PM."

We both laugh and go into the kitchen for snacks and wine, and then take our food out onto the back porch. Rebecca fills me in on how her kids are doing and any drama I missed on the Wilson side of the family. We're related through marriage, not blood, but that didn't stop her from welcoming me into the family.

"So tell me about your life." She takes another sip of wine. "What's new?"

"Nothing really."

She raises her eyebrows. "You're young and pretty. I need to live vicariously through you. Tell me you stayed out past midnight last night and watched a movie with at least a PG-13 rating."

"I did stay out late last night. Grandpa had a friend over." I make a face and shudder, causing Rebecca to laugh. "So I went to Getaway and hung out there. At the place I work on my day off. My life really isn't that exciting."

"Interesting you chose to go to Getaway."

"It's the only place open after ten PM around here, and I didn't want to go home and risk walking in on something I'd never be able to unsee."

"You could have come here. Or gone to Quinn's."

"She was at the bar too."

Rebecca fills our glasses up again. "Mm-hm. It had nothing to do with the company you keep at Getaway. Not at all."

"Yeah, I like Logan and Owen. They're great guys and fun to hang out with."

"They are two good-looking men. I don't blame you for wanting to get a little extra time with them."

"Diana emailed me about her wedding today." I change the subject. "I'm only allowed to bring a *serious* plus one."

"What does that even mean?"

"I have no idea. A long-term boyfriend? A husband? All I know is I really don't want to go to that wedding alone. She's going to pair me up with another single guest in the hotel room. That's not awkward at all."

Rebecca tosses back her glass of wine and runs her eyes over me. She's scheming something, I can tell by the slight smile on her face.

"Whatever you're thinking, no."

"You haven't even heard what I'm thinking."

I raise my eyebrows. "Fine. What are you thinking?"

"Don't go to the wedding alone. Bring someone."

"But I don't have a boyfriend, let alone a serious one."

She reaches for the wine again only to realize the bottle is empty. "You haven't seen your family in like a year. They don't know what's going on in your life."

My lips start to curve into a smile. "That is a good point. I could be engaged for all they know."

"Tell them that and enjoy the weekend in Hawaii. Lord knows you deserve a break."

"Okay…so I tell Diana that I'm engaged and am bringing my fiancé. Where exactly do you find a fiancé for hire? A Craigslist ad? I'll make sure to put that murderers need not apply."

Rebecca laughs. "I think you can hire a male escort. Or at least that's what they'd do in the romantic comedy movies."

"Sounds expensive." I shake my head. "I'll just have to woman-up and tell Diana I'm still very much single and can—" I cut off when my phone rings. I pull it out of my purse and look up at Rebecca. "Speak of the Devil. It's my mother."

I take a big gulp of wine before I answer. Mom texts me a few times a month to check in on me but has only called a handful of times since I moved here.

"Mom, hi," I say into the phone, sounding way too enthusiastic. "How are you?"

"Hello, honey. I'm good, thank you. Did you get your sister's email?"

I wince. "Uh, yeah. And I replied."

"She said she sent you one more after that. I supposed you didn't bother checking. Our meeting with the caterer for the final tasting got bumped up to tomorrow morning. I need to give him the final count. I should put you down for one, I presume."

"Uh," I start, feeling her judgment weigh down on me. It's impressive, really, how she can be so condescending with so few words. "No. I'm bringing a date."

Rebecca squeals in the background, and I wave my hand at

her to shoo her away. Clamping her hand over her mouth, she goes into the house to get more wine.

"A date? Each plate costs well over a hundred dollars. If this *date* is just some fling, you might not be with a month from now—"

"We're engaged."

A few seconds of silence tick by. "What?"

"He's, uh, my fiancé," I say right as Rebecca comes back out, almost spilling the wine as she does an excited dance around the porch.

"W-when did this happen?" Mom stammers. "Why didn't you tell us?"

"It, uh, happened recently, and I didn't want to steal the spotlight from Diana. I know how big of a deal this wedding is for her."

"It is a big deal, but so is you getting engaged. Who is this man? How did you meet? What does your ring look like?"

"What, Mom?" I shout. "I can't hear you. I think I'm losing service. I'm driving through a cornfield right now. Yep. Can't hear a thing. Talk to you later. Love you!"

I hang up and feel the blood leave my face. "I think she bought it. Grab your computer and let's look for—" I shudder "—male escorts."

Rebecca twists the cap off the Moscato and pours a bit in her glass before disappearing inside, returning a minute later with her laptop. "What do we even type in?" she asks, pulling up a search engine.

"Male escorts for hire? Legal ones. I do not want to get arrested for prostitution."

"That's always a good thing to avoid." She types in the search, and we filter through results. The first site we check out is promising, and they have a few escorts located in the Chicago area.

"Ohhh, Stephan is a hottie!" I point to a dark-haired guy.

Rebecca clicks on his profile, and we ogle over his shirtless pictures for a minute before checking his rates.

"Seventy-five hundred bucks for a weekend?" I blink, making sure I'm reading that right. "I should have been an escort."

"You're pretty enough."

"Maybe I'll consider it."

"I'm pretty sure most people do expect sex, even though it says that's a hard limit on the website."

"Way to crush my dreams." I shake my head. "Okay, let's see if we can find one who's not as good-looking. Maybe they'll have a lower rate."

None do, and I can't afford to drop several grand on some stranger who's supposed to fool my family into thinking we're so in love and anxiously awaiting our own wedding date.

Rebecca closes the computer. "I was thinking…you could ask someone you're already friends with."

"All my friends are—no way. I'm not asking Logan."

"Why not? You're friends, right?"

I grip the stem of my wine glass, looking at the Moscato sloshing around inside. "Of course we are."

"Then I don't see what the problem is."

The problems are endless, starting with the way he runs his hand through his hair, messing it up, which looks so sexy on him. Another problem is how fit and tan he is, and the way his muscles flexed as he moved those pavers today. The way sweat rolled down said muscles, practically forcing my eyes to check out his chiseled abdomen. But that's not as problematic as the sharp V cut of muscle that disappears down his waistband.

Or the way that he's both equally grumpy and one of the most thoughtful people on the planet, which makes him infuriatingly desirable.

"I guess there isn't a problem." I smile, bringing the glass of wine to my lips to try and cover up the color rushing to my cheeks. "Assuming he'd want to go with me."

"It's a free trip to Hawaii. Who wouldn't want to go?"

"Someone sane."

She playfully nudges me. "Just ask him. The worst he can say is no."

Logan and I know each other well enough that we could easily pull off pretending to be a real couple. But Rebecca is wrong. Saying no isn't the worst thing that can happen.

The worst will be him agreeing. Because I don't know how well I can fake the feelings for him that I don't want to admit I have.

CHAPTER 5

LOGAN

"Hey." Danielle takes her purse off her shoulder as she walks through the back door of the bar. We're getting ready to open, and she just got here for her shift. The heavy door closes with a whoosh behind her, sending her hair flying around her face. She reaches up to tame it, and the light yellow fabric of her sundress stretches up over her breasts. She's not wearing a bra, and I can see the faint outline of her nipple through the fabric.

I swallow hard, talk down my dick, and look away.

"Hey," I say back. "You look nice."

"Thanks. I'd say the same to you, but I don't want to lie." She flashes a grin and walks past me and into the office to put her purse away. I readjust the heavy box of booze I'm carrying, trying —and failing—to keep my thoughts PG.

"You look nice?" Owen stands in the threshold of the kitchen, shaking his head. "At this point, I don't think you even want out of the friendzone."

Ignoring him, I breeze right past and set the box down on the counter next to the walk-in refrigerator.

"I'm genuinely concerned for you," Owen goes on. "When was the last time you got any pussy?"

It was a while ago, and he damn well knows it. The blind hookups were fun in our early twenties, but now it's lost its appeal. Even before I met Danielle, I started feeling the longing to settle down, to have something serious and think about starting a family. I always knew I'd get married and have kids, but it always seemed so far away and out of reach.

Maybe it just took the right girl to give me that final shove out of the bachelor lifestyle.

"You do still like pussy right?" Owen goes on. "Or have you forgotten what it feels like to fuck all together?"

I give him a glare.

"I'll help you out tonight." He leans against the wall, watching me open the box and start moving the beer into the fridge. "I'll do the work, get you a chick who wants to hook up, and then we can pull the old twin-switch."

"I'll pass, thanks."

"What? Afraid they'll know it's you the moment you fail to live up to the expectations I set?" He grins, proud of himself and thinking he's actually being clever.

"I wonder how we're related some days."

Owen laughs. "Then why don't you take Danielle home? Oh wait. You did. And you bored her to death, and she passed out on the couch."

My jaw tenses when I think about that night. Of the way her soft and supple breasts felt pressed up against my chest. How her hair fell like a curtain over us both. Blood rushes to my cock, and I shift my weight, trying to derail my thoughts.

Because right now, they're headed to a place of no return.

Just having her against me like that felt so fucking good. Kissing her would be even better. I blink and see her full lips in front of me as her tongue darts out and wets them both. I don't think she was even aware of what she was doing as she leaned in closer and closer, as neither of us could resist the pull.

I clear my throat. "She's said multiple times that she doesn't want to date anyone until she gets her life together."

Owen raises his eyebrows. "What does that even mean?"

My shoulders rise and fall in a shrug as I grab a few more beers to shelve. "Hell if I know. Maybe go back to grad school and get some fancy job?"

"Even I know that's bullshit. She hated her life back in Greenwich. And you're not just anyone. You happen to look just like me, and I'm one handsome fellow."

I roll my eyes but end up laughing at Owen. "I can't argue with that, even though we both know I'm the better-looking one. And I'm smarter."

"Keep telling yourself that." Owen claps me on the back and leaves the kitchen, probably going to the bar to pour himself a drink and not actually do any work. I keep restocking the shelves as the bar opens, and a few of our regulars come in the second that neon *open* sign is turned on.

Opening for lunch on the weekends is a new thing for us and was Danielle's idea. When Owen and I bought the place, it was purely a bar. We added the kitchen and slowly expanded the menu over the years. Transitioning from Getaway, just a bar, to Getaway Bar and Grill was something we had in mind from day one, but put off executing it until Danielle laid everything out in a rather impressive presentation. We make a lot of money just from lunch and dinner orders alone, and the food here is pretty fucking good if I do say so myself.

"Got plans for the weekend?" I ask Danielle.

"Oh, of course. I've got my calendar completely booked," she laughs. "Which really means I'll probably end up watching Netflix while scooping up egg salad from a bowl with cheese Pringles. Which I totally didn't do last night."

"That's an interesting combination."

"It was surprisingly good. I mean, I assume it would be if it weren't too disgusting for me to try." She flashes a pretty smile, and I'm back to needing a cold shower.

"How's the job search going?"

She's about to answer when one of our regulars walks up to the bar. "Hey, George." She reaches under the bar for a glass. "Don't tell me. Let me try to read your mind." She sets the glass on the counter and closes her eyes. "An Old Fashioned and a side order of cheese fries."

George gasps, throwing out his hands in fake shock. He orders the same thing every time he comes in, which is nearly every day. He's a bit of a local legend around here, but his tale of war hero turned drunk doesn't have the happy ending we all hoped for. Still, he's as respected as he can be, and is one of the more polite drunks we have sitting at the bar day in and day out.

"I don't know how you do it!"

Danielle laughs and starts making his drink. "It's a gift. You know I almost considered running away and joining the circus as a psychic as a kid." She finishes his drink and brings it over. "How are the grandkids? Have you been going over to see them like we talked about?"

For someone who doesn't plan to stay in Eastwood for long, she sure gets along well here. I step away, getting a beer for another regular, and then go to one of the tables to take a food order and bring it to the kitchen. We're going on two months of opening early, and we've been consistently busy. If things keep going the way they are, we plan on hiring another waitress or two as well as more help in the kitchen. Never in a million years did I think we'd make this much more just by opening in the early afternoon.

And it's all thanks to Danielle.

"Uh-oh." George slurps his drink. "The Sheriff is here. You up to no good again?" he asks Danielle.

She gives him a wink. "Always."

Knowing my brother always stops in on Fridays to take food home for lunch, I already put in his order. I go back into the kitchen and grab it.

"Thanks," he says and looks around. "It's crowded already."

"Yeah." My eyes go to Danielle, watching her smile as she talks to Tommy Oaken. He's leaning over the bar, eyes flitting away from Danielle's to stare at her tits. "It was a good idea to open for lunch. We might start opening early on weekdays too."

She laughs, reaching out to touch his arm. Something tightens in my stomach. I clench my jaw and look away. I'm not jealous. There's nothing to be jealous of, right?

Dammit.

I've never been a good liar.

"Logan?" Wes repeats in a tone that lets me know he's said my name more than once.

"Yeah?" I turn my attention back to Wes, and a small smile plays on his lips as he follows my gaze. He's not one to meddle and is my only sibling who hasn't given me shit over my lack of relationship with Danielle. But that look in his eyes is almost as bad as Quinn and Scarlet forcing us under mistletoe three times last Christmas.

"Never mind." He takes the bag of takeout and gets up to leave but turns back to face me. "You're smart. Second smartest in the family after Quinn. So stop being stupid."

CHAPTER 6

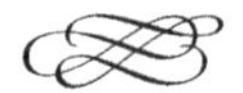

DANIELLE

I'm fairly sure the reason the universe never granted me magical powers is because it knew I'd use them in nefarious ways. Like that speeding ticket I got a few weeks ago? I'd make the cop think he was giving me a ticket when all he was handing me was a blank sheet of paper. The shoes I've been eyeing but can't afford would ring up at half the price and no one would be none the wiser.

And this guy sitting in front of me?

This lying, cheating, slimy bastard?

I'd turn him into a rat. No...that's an insult to rodents everywhere. They're kind of cute with their little whiskers and the way they hold things in their tiny hands when they eat.

Maybe I'd turn him into a worm. Oh—no, I've got a better idea. A stink bug that just happens to be flying over the freeway when a semi-truck barrels down the road and smacks right into him, smearing him all over the—well, now I know why I don't have cool powers.

I turn away from the table, fake smile disappearing from my face the moment my back is turned. James Hills has a wife. A wife who just found out she's expecting a baby boy. I know because she told me when I saw her at the farmer's market just a few days ago.

"Getting comfy over there?" Logan asks, eyes going to Tommy, who's sitting at the bar, and then back to me.

"What?"

"You two seemed friendly."

I wrinkle my nose. "I guess? I talk to all my customers. I get better tips that way."

"Yeah." He raises his eyebrows. "You sure it's just for tips?"

Logan gets moody like this every now and then, and usually I dismiss it until he's back to normal. But today I feel like pushing.

"Yeah, for tips. I'm not exactly making bank as a bartender, and I'm trying to build my savings." I put my hand on my hip and take a deep breath, making my breasts rise and fall under my dress. "But if I didn't know better, I'd say you were jealous."

"Jealous," he snorts. "Jealous of Tommy Oaken. That guy's a loser."

"Then you won't care if I go on a date with him tomorrow night?"

"You're working tomorrow night."

"Then the next day." I keep my face neutral, reading Logan's expression. I don't have a date with Tommy, nor do I want one. But he did ask me out, which is more than I can say for Logan. Maybe I should go out with Tommy just to get back out there in the dating game.

"Fine," Logan huffs. "At least you'd be going out with someone."

He gathers a few empty glasses and takes them back into the kitchen to put them in the sink.

"What's that supposed to mean?" I ask, following behind him.

"It means you've been swearing up and down since the moment you got here that you hate men and don't want to date anyone."

"I never said I hate men. I think. I mean, I might have. Because guys are jerks."

"We're not all jerks," he spits, eyes clouding with anger. "By all means, go out with Tommy fucking Oaken. But if you want to date a guy who's *not* a jerk, then don't go out with that fucker." Logan goes into the walk-in fridge, slamming the door shut behind him. Balling my fingers into fists, I march right in after him.

"Why do you care who I go out with?"

"Seriously?" He puts the cut of hamburger meat he was holding back onto the shelf.

"Yeah." I let out a breath and feel a chill creep down my back already.

Logan's eyes drill into mine with a fire I've never seen before. It cuts right through me, chilling me more than the cold air billowing around us. He strides forward, and I step back, pinning myself against the closed door of the fridge. Cold metal kisses my skin, and goosebumps break out along my flesh.

Logan doesn't stop until his hips are right up against mine. My lips part and I inhale, but I still get no air. His face is inches from mine, and I can't take my eyes off his lips.

"What are we?" he asks.

I slowly shake my head. "We're uh, friends?"

"That's all you want?"

"Yeah. You're my best friend, Logan. What's wrong with that?" I hate the words that are coming out of my mouth, but admitting I want more, that I could easily fall in love with him, terrifies me.

"Maybe I am stupid," he starts, tipping his head down. "Or maybe I've been too fucking nice." He brings one arm up, bicep flexing, and pushes my hair back over my shoulder.

"What are you talking about?" My voice comes out thin, and my breath clouds around us.

"You know exactly what I'm talking about. And I don't want to do this anymore."

My eyes flutter closed, and I inhale again, trying to fill my lungs with oxygen because suddenly I can't remember how to breathe. A warmth spreads through me, starting in my stomach and rushing over every inch of me. It settles between my legs, and the longing I've felt for Logan Dawson, the feelings I've ignored and pushed away, threaten to break down the gates.

"Then don't," I whisper.

Just when I think Logan is going to kiss me, when I can let my body finally cave into what I've been craving since the moment I laid eyes on Logan, he pushes off the door and goes back to the shelf.

Blinking, I bring my arms up and wrap them around myself, unable to stop shivering now. With an armload of beer I know we don't need to put in the mini fridge at the bar, Logan storms toward the door. I move out of the way, still not sure exactly what happened.

Or what didn't.

And I can't help the sinking feeling that I just fucked up any sort of chance I had with Logan.

~

"Can you believe that guy?" I narrow my eyes, watching James reach across the table and take the pretty, young blonde's hand.

"What's wrong with him?" Owen asks, looking up from the bar. Logan has kept himself busy doing anything he can that involves avoiding me.

"He has a wife. And that is not her."

"What an ass."

"Shouldn't we do something?"

Owen cocks an eyebrow. "What do you expect to do? We're not the moral police."

"Yeah, but look at him. His wife is pregnant, and now his lips are on that lady's hand. Maybe she doesn't know he's married."

"He's not wearing his wedding ring. She probably doesn't."

"Isn't that even more of a reason to…I don't know…kick him out?"

"He's ordered three drinks with top shelf liquor already. I'm not kicking him out."

"Fine." I put my little pad of paper and pencil into my apron pocket. "I'll do it."

"Danielle," Owen starts and reaches for my wrist. His fingers close around it, and while his hand is identical to Logan's, his touch does nothing to me. It's not electric. Doesn't send a shiver down my spine or make a million butterflies take flight in my stomach. "We can't kick him out for being a douchebag."

"Well, you should."

He lets go of my wrist and offers a sympathetic smile. Logan is the only one who knows the full details of why I left home, but Owen knows the Cliff's Notes version.

"I shouldn't encourage you," he grumbles. "But wait until he's paid. Then go ask how his wife is doing."

A smile takes over my face. "You really are the evil twin."

Owen gives me an over-the-top wink. "I wear that title proudly." He shifts his gaze to Logan, and while I know they haven't had time to talk yet today, I'm sure he's aware something is up with him. It's hard for me to grasp the whole "it's a twin thing" when I have a shitty relationship with my sister, but those two are in sync without even trying.

I don't want things to be weird between Logan *and* Owen. A sour feeling sinks heavily in my stomach. It's one I'm all too familiar with. It starts as a slight stomach ache and ends with anxiety wrapping around me like an itchy sweater that clings to me, suffocating me, making my fingers tremble and my mind race.

The only way I know how to shut it off is with a shot of

something dark and strong. Not a healthy coping mechanism, I know. It's been a while since I felt the all-consuming anxiety, and it was one of the things I swore I'd avoid when moving to Eastwood.

My plan was to work hard, keep my head down, legs shut, and figure my shit out so I could get back on track.

Trouble is, I have no idea where that track leads or if I even want to get back on it.

I wait on a few more tables, running around like crazy to make drinks, take orders to the kitchen, and bring out food. We're definitely going to have to hire people, which is a good problem to have.

Keeping an eye on Mr. Infidelity, I take out another tray of food and then stop by James to collect his tab. He paid in cash and told me to keep the change.

Score.

"How's the pregnancy treating your wife?" I ask, folding the bills and slipping them into my apron pocket. "She was absolutely glowing when I saw her last week." I flash a pretty smile and step back. Owen leans over the bar, entertained as he watches everything play out.

The pretty blonde who looks like she could easily be a Daisy or a Candy, jerks her hand out of James's grasp.

"You're married?"

Yep, poor girl didn't know.

"I…I…it's not like that," James stammers, but it's too late. Blondie gets up, throws her drink in his face and storms out of the bar. James sits there, stunned, as diet Coke rolls down his chin. Then he looks around, realizes everyone is looking at him, and hurries out of the bar, calling after the blonde.

Her name *is* Candy.

Feeling like I did my part to save at least one person from a cheating asshat, I grab my purse, the salad I packed, and head outside to take my break. It's hot again today, and I love the heat.

I exit through the back of the bar and sit on the little stoop, stretching my legs out in the sun.

I'm halfway through my salad when gravel crunches under someone's feet. I look up, expecting to see Dean, Archer, or even Quinn, since they usually park around back and come in through this door. But instead of a friendly face, I'm greeted with a scowl.

"You fucking whore," James sneers as he stumbles toward me. Right, he's had several strong drinks already.

"You're the whore," I retort, putting the lid back on my salad before I set it down. Priorities, right?

"She called my wife," he slurs.

"Not my problem." I loop my arm through my purse strap and stand, reaching back for the door. My heart speeds up, and I'm well aware how dangerous a situation I'm in right now. James is drunk, and now he's desperate and angry.

I need to punch in a code to get back into the bar, and that requires me turning away from James so I can look at the keypad. But I feel like if I break eye contact, he'll use that time to rush at me, attacking like a wild animal.

Sweat drips down my back, and the itchy anxiety sweater is now a zip-up onesie. With footies. And a hood that's pulled tight around my face. The ties are wrapping around my neck, making it hard to breathe.

"My wife wants to leave me now." James comes closer. "And take my child with her."

"You…you should have thought about that before you cheated on her." It takes great effort to keep my voice level. My fingers shake, and I blindly hit buttons, thinking I got the combination right.

I didn't.

I get two more tries before it'll lock me out for five minutes. I don't have five minutes.

James narrows his eyes and balls his fist. "You're going to pay for this, bitch."

I sidestep back, bumping into the wall. Then the door flies open and Logan jumps out, shoving James hard in the chest. James takes a swing at Logan, who blocks the blow and pops James square in the nose.

"What the fuck is the matter with you?" Logan shouts, taking one of James's arms and twisting it behind his back. "I should beat the shit out of you for even thinking about hitting a woman."

He pulls James's arm back further and then shoves him down into the grass.

"Logan...Thank you," I say in a shaky voice. I look at him, and all he does is flick his eyes to up mine. "Do you want me to call Wes?"

"I got this."

"I can—"

"Just go back inside." He looks back at James, who's too drunk to upright himself now that he's down, reminding me of a turtle on its back.

"Logan," I start, heart sinking. The anxiety onesie is back, but this time it's wrapping me up in an extra blanket of dread and regret. Logan lifts his head, eyes meeting mine.

I should see anger. Hell, I want to see anger. Because knowing he's pissed at me would hurt a lot less than the disappointment and hurt I see reflected in his deep brown eyes. Disappointment I know my words caused him.

My words I wish I could take back. Because as much as it scares me to admit, Logan Dawson has my heart.

CHAPTER 7

DANIELLE

I stick my fork into the cake and rest my head against the kitchen cabinet. I trade the fork for a bottle of wine and take a big gulp. I need it to wash down the taste of carrot cake. Normally, I steer clear of this stuff, but it was the only cake Walmart had in their bakery at one AM.

Feeling sick from all the cream cheese frosting, I close the cake box, wipe my eyes, and push myself up off the kitchen floor. I drop my fork in the sink, take the wine, and go out onto the back porch, wanting the quiet of the night to open up and swallow me whole.

Sundance is looking out his Dutch door, head hanging low and his lips slack. He's nearly asleep, but he perks up and nickers softly when he sees me. I chug another mouthful of wine, grab a pair of flip-flops, and walk through the damp grass to the corral. I spill a bit of the wine when I climb through the wooden fence, and Sundance tries to lick it off my arm when I get to his stall.

"I've made a mess of things again," I tell him, resting my head against his. He nudges me, trying to get to the bottle of wine. "I'm throwing a pity party for one and drinking my problems away. You're a horse. What do you have to be anxious about?"

I undo the latch and open the door to his stall, squinting in the dark to avoid stepping in a fresh pile of horse poo as I move through his stall and into the barn. I stick my arm through the bars on his interior door, undoing another latch, and go into the aisle. Blindly, I walk through the barn until I come to the cross ties. Then I reach out in front of me for the string to pull to turn the light on.

"Sorry, guys," I say to Bailey and Alibi, the other two horses. All three are Quarter Horses with similar levels of training. Sundance is the most ornery of the bunch, which is probably why he's my favorite. His coat is dark chestnut, and he has a thick white blaze on his face.

I take another drink of wine and grab a towel from the cross ties. Shaking it out to make sure there are no spiders, I fold it in two and lay it down in the aisle next to Sundance's stall.

I was never a horse person before I came here. Mom made sure both Diana and I took lessons for a few years, if only to say that her girls took riding lessons at one of more prestigious barns in Greenwich. Everything was done for show. I didn't get it then like I do now.

Horses are big and heavy, with four feet that end in solid hooves. They could kill you in seconds if they wanted to. Putting your faith and trust into an animal this powerful seems like a death wish, doesn't it? But they trust you back.

And that bond is something I still can't explain, yet here I am, drinking wine from the bottle while talking to Sundance. People on the east coast would pay good money for this kind of therapy.

"Telling Mom I was engaged was stupid. I can't hire an escort, and I'm pretty sure they're going think I want sex, and I don't. Not even from Stephan and his perfect abs that I'm pretty sure were photoshopped into that photo." I take another drink of wine. "And the one guy that might have agreed to play the part doesn't want anything to do with me right now."

I let out a sigh and rest my head against the wooden stall. "I'm going to have to tell Mom that I either made up the fiancé thing, pretend like we had a very dramatic break-up, or try to convince everyone he wasn't able to get off work."

I let out a breath and swat away mosquitos.

"I think I get it now. I'm still trying. Trying to fit in. Trying to follow their rules. Well, fuck their rules." I raise the bottle of wine, toasting myself.

Sundance sticks his head over the stall guard and noses for the wine again. I get up and get him a treat, which of course makes the others want treats too. I toss a treat in everyone's food buckets and then give Sundance a hug goodnight. I lock up the barn and go back inside, feeling a bit lighter.

Quietly, I sneak through the house and up to my room. I change into PJs and climb into bed, trying to tell myself it'll be all right in the morning. I don't work tomorrow, and by the time I see Logan again, enough time will have passed that things won't be awkward anymore.

It has to.

Going against my better judgment, I grab my phone and send Logan one of the better Game of Thrones memes I've been saving. There's a chance he's sleeping, but then the text goes from *delivered* to *read*, and I hate that he never disabled that feature on his phone. Because now I'm going to stare at my phone for the rest of the night waiting for him to reply.

I exit out of my texts and check my email. This time, there really is another job rejection letter in there, telling me that while my resumé is impressive, I lack the experience the company is looking for.

How the heck am I supposed to get experience when no one will hire me? Though, if I'm being honest with myself, I'm glad I didn't get that job. The office is down in Indianapolis, and the thought of leaving Eastwood makes me a little sad.

I black out the screen of my phone and set it on the nightstand. Orange Cat paws at my door, and I throw back the covers to let him in. He runs away as soon as the door is open.

"Jerk," I grumble and fall back into bed. Closing my eyes, I think of Grandpa's words: *how lucky you that you get to fail.*

I'm still trying to feel lucky.

~

I CLIMB UP THE BASEMENT STAIRS AND EMERGE INTO THE NARROW hall that runs behind the kitchen at Getaway. It's Monday, about an hour before we open, and I just finished inventorying our hard liquor supply. I haven't seen Logan since Friday, and he never responded to my text.

The air is different now, and it's slowly eating away at me. I would give anything to go back to that moment in the fridge and kiss him instead of waiting for him to kiss me.

"I got everything counted," I say and extend the clipboard, heart in my throat.

"Thanks." He takes the clipboard from me and sets it on the desk. "Now I can see how much to take out of Owen's paycheck."

I smile, just wanting things to go back to normal between us. "I'm pretty sure you can take out at least two bottles of Patron and a handful of beers."

Logan chuckles and plants his feet on the ground, pushing the rolling chair back to the printer, grabbing the paper that it spits out. He spins the chair around and looks at me, really looks at me. My lips part and my pulse speeds up, getting a flash of his body against mine, the heat of his skin contrasting with the cold metal of the fridge.

I feel color rush to my cheeks, and I look away, taking a strand of hair and twisting it between my fingers.

"How's, uh, Dexter?"

Logan shakes his head. "The little shit pulled a carton of eggs off the counter this morning and ate half of them before anyone noticed."

I laugh. "Have fun smelling those farts tonight."

Logan laughs too and plows a hand through his hair. "I'll put him in Owen's room."

I smile, and it would be easy to tell myself things are going back to normal, but there's still a distance in Logan's eyes that's tearing me up inside.

We both go back to work, getting ready to open. With the exception of our regulars, Mondays are pretty slow until about five or six in the evening. Though today, we did get a handful of people coming in, confused as to why we're not open for lunch on weekdays when we are on weekends. I keep track of it all to use to prove to Logan and Owen that turning this place into a full-on bar and grill will be more than worth it. There are a few other restaurants in Eastwood and only one other diner. We're on opposite sides of the town, and a decent amount of highway traffic comes through our doors. We'd do really well serving food during the day.

I'm jotting down an informal business proposal when the overwhelming smell of Chanel No. 5 wafts through the doors. It's breezy today, and every time the front doors open, a warm summer wind comes through. I'm sure it's annoying the people at the tables near the door, but I find it refreshing, especially when you consider that the few regulars glued to their barstools aren't the cleanest.

I look up just in time to see my sister step away from Peter's side, heading to the bathroom. Peter looks around the bar, and his eyes settle on me. He brings his hand up in a little wave, and I do the mature thing and drop down to the floor, crouching behind the bar.

Maybe if he can't see me, he'll go away.

"Danielle?" His voice comes from above me. I've never wished for a cream pie more than I do right now. I'd stick my face in it and pop up, speaking with an accent Mrs. Doubtfire style. I don't have a pie, but I can still pretend I don't know him…right?

"I'm sorry," I say with the worst British accent in the world as I stand up. "I think you're mistaking me for someone else."

Logan, who's at the other side of the bar, looks up. "What the hell?" he mouths, and I only respond by wrinkling my nose.

Peter tips his head, looking me up and down. He's checking me out, and he's not trying to hide it.

"You look good, Danielle."

"I told you, I'm not Danielle. I'm, uh, Kasey, and I've never heard of this Danielle before." My accent is starting to sound Scottish. And now, both Peter and Logan are looking at me like I've lost my damn mind. Truth is, I did a long time ago.

"Dani!" Diana calls, coming out of the bathroom. She must have just gone in to check out her hair or something. She's beaming, but the smile isn't genuine.

"What are you doing here?" I blurt.

"Nice to see you too." She presses her lips together and adjusts the strap of her Louis Vuitton purse over her shoulder.

"Of course it's nice to see *you*." It's not good to see Peter, and they both know exactly how I feel. "I just wasn't expecting it. At all."

"Peter has business in Chicago tomorrow, so we came a day early and thought we'd drive down and see how you're faring in this little town."

"I'm doing all right. I like it here."

She raises her eyebrows. "It seems like it could be relaxing with that slower pace of life. And I have to say, it's nice to see that you've stopped caring what people think of you."

"What?"

Her eyes drop to my crop top. "Oh, never mind."

"Can I get you something to drink?"

"A hot water with lemon, please."

I'm positive no one has ever walked through the doors of Getaway and ordered that before. "Uh, sure."

"So." Diana slides into a barstool. "Mom said you told her you're bringing a date to my wedding."

"Uh, yeah. I am." Is it just me or is the temperature rising in this place? I can see Logan watching me out of the corner of my eye.

"And that's not all she said. So, let me see it."

"See what?"

"Your ring, silly! You're bringing your fiancé, right?"

Now I need some hot water with lemon because my throat is suddenly dry. "I, uh…"

"Did you make it up?" Diana's lips curve into a smirk, waiting to bust me. "Because I wouldn't blame you. I mean, your big sis is getting married, and it will be the wedding of the year. A little lie wouldn't be a surprise."

"I didn't make it up," I stammer.

"Well, then show me your ring."

"I, uh, I…"

Diana grabs my left hand and brings it to her face.

Dammit.

CHAPTER 8

LOGAN

I've never so much as seen a photo of Danielle's sister, but I know that woman standing there has to be her. They look alike, with the exact same shade of blue-green eyes. Her sister's are heavily lined in dark liner, topped with fake lashes so long it's a wonder she can see anything in front of her.

Danielle stammers but holds her ground.

"Well, then show me your ring," her sister spits in a tone that borders on mocking. She knows Danielle isn't really engaged and made the whole thing up. I have no idea why she did, but I'm sure it was for a good reason. Her family is judgmental and cares about appearances.

Maybe her parents were pressuring her to come back home so they could set her up with another rich asshole. The thought of Danielle going on a date with some trust fund jerk makes jealousy bubble in my stomach. I need to stop giving a fuck.

Danielle only wants to be friends.

"I, uh, I…"

Diana snatches Danielle's hand and lets out a snort of laughter. This is exactly the type of thing Diana will never let Danielle live down, and I can see the panic in Danielle's eyes, which is out of character for her and I don't like it.

I want to stay neutral in all of this and not get involved. But, dammit, I can't sit back and watch Danielle struggle like this. She's tough even though she doesn't realize it. She stands up for what she believes in, even if that means upsetting a few people.

She thinks her life is a mess, but it's one hell of a beautiful mess if that's the case.

No one can unnerve you like your family can, and right now, she's fumbling bad. Why she lied about being engaged doesn't matter. What matters is she's my friend, even though I long for more.

"What's that?" the jerk who I assume is Peter asks, eyes dropped to Danielle's chest. Blood rushes to Danielle's cheeks, and I can't stand this anymore.

I don't think. I just act.

"Did you forget your ring again, honey?" I dart around the bar and over to Danielle. "She does it all the time. Takes it off when she's out in the barn with the horses and forgets to put it back on."

Diana's eyes flutter, and it's a surprise those ridiculously long lashes don't tangle and get stuck together. Danielle's shoulders relax, and she spins around, eyes meeting mine. The look of relief in them makes my heart do a stupid skip-a-beat thing.

"You're right, babe!" She giggles and reaches up to touch my arm but hesitates for just a second before putting her delicate fingers on my bicep. "I'm always so worried about losing it in the barn I take it off. It's safe and sound in my jewelry box in my room."

I smile down at her, carefully bringing one hand up and resting it on her waist. She's wearing a crop-top today, and my fingers grace her warm, smooth skin. She tenses, but I don't think it's because she's uncomfortable by my touch.

"I told you we should just get matching tattoos instead."

Danielle laughs, and this time it's more like her normal laugh. Her grip on my arm tightens a bit. "Right, as long as yours says *property of Danielle* so everyone knows you're mine."

"I wouldn't have it any other way," I laugh and look into her eyes. She holds my gaze, silently thanking me, and then turns around, facing her sister.

"This is Logan. Logan, this is my sister Diana." She purposely didn't introduce Peter, and I'm half tempted to act like I don't notice him. For two weeks straight, Owen and I acted like Quinn was invisible when we were kids. We played the part so well Quinn actually thought no one could see her...which got her into trouble when she tried sneaking around.

"You're engaged to him?" Diana's eyebrows go up even higher.

"Yeah, why? What were you expecting?"

Her sister shakes her head. "A cowboy, I guess. Definitely not someone who looks like they—"

"Tend bars," Peter interrupts. "Which is what you do, right? I'd like to order a drink, actually."

"Logan owns this place," Danielle says. "And I tend the bar. You got an issue with that?" She cocks an eyebrow, testing him.

That's my girl.

"So, go ahead and take a seat if you'd like to order. I'll bring out the hot water and lemon in just a minute." She waves her hand at an empty table. Diana and Peter walk away, and Danielle grabs my arm, pulling me into the kitchen.

"Thank you, Logan, so much." She lets out a shaky breath.

"Why does your sister think you're engaged?"

Danielle winces, and her cheeks redden again. She has no poker face, and it's so fucking charming. "Her wedding is coming up, and I never sent in the RSVP. She emailed me and made a point to say I'm only allowed to bring a 'serious' plus-one, and if I didn't have one, I'd be paired up in a hotel room with some other random single guest. Then my mom called and was being judgey and condescending as normal without even trying. She said she was marking me down as single, and I just blurted out I was engaged."

"Wow."

She lets out a breath, shoulders sagging. "I know. Thanks again…but I don't want to drag you into any family drama. It's like quicksand. Once you fall in, you can't get out, and then you're just waiting for the slow release of death. By sand? Does it kill you by crushing you? Or from the lack of oxygen?"

"I think the latter."

"That makes sense." She wrinkles her nose. "That would be awful. But not as bad as telling my mom the truth."

I look at her pretty face, mind racing. She told her mom she's engaged and is bringing a date to the wedding. Her sister already thinks I'm her fiancé. What's the harm in continuing the lie?

"Don't tell her the truth," I blurt before I have a chance to think about what I'm saying. That's been my issue all along. I've overthought every damn move I've made. I've almost grabbed and kissed Danielle more times than I can count, and I've stopped myself every time, thinking about the ways things could go wrong.

But what if they go right?

"She's going to wonder when I show up alone in Hawaii."

I reach my hand out, brushing a strand of Danielle's hair back behind her ear. "I guess I'm going to Hawaii with you."

Her lips part and she stares at me like I'm crazy. Which I am. I'm completely and totally crazy about my best friend. Swallowing hard, I let my hand fall. "I mean, if you want me to."

"Yes. Just don't go falling in love with me, Dawson." She bites her lip. "I…I actually wanted to ask you to come with me before but didn't think you'd want to."

"I've never been to Hawaii," I start. "And I've always wanted to go." I give her a crooked smile. "And you're paying, right?"

"Paying to take you to Hawaii is a lot cheaper than what the escort would have charged."

I let out a snort of laughter. "You were going to hire an escort to take to Hawaii with you?"

"It crossed my mind until I realized they charge over five grand for a weekend."

"Damn. I went into the wrong business. Well, not so much me. But Owen…he'd have his weekends double-booked and would pull it off."

"I promise never to mention it to him."

"Good idea. Better to play it safe."

She lets out another sigh and grabs a coffee mug, filling it with hot water. Adding a wedge of lemon to the saucer, she takes it out to her sister. I check on a few of the other customers and then get flagged down by Diana. Danielle is seated at their table, and I come over, taking a spot next to Danielle.

"So, how'd you two meet?" Diana asks.

"Danielle came into the bar," I start, telling the complete truth, "her first night in Eastwood. I saw her walk through the door and knew I was a goner." I flick my eyes to Danielle. She doesn't know I'm telling the truth, though.

"I started working here," Danielle goes on. "And we hit it off right away."

A real couple would kiss or hug or at the very least touch each other right now. I take a breath and then put my hand on Danielle's. She flips her hand over, lacing her fingers through mine.

It's unnerving how natural this feels.

"How long are you staying in town?" I ask Diana. She needs to leave before someone blows our cover.

"Not that long. We have to head back to Chicago soon," she replies quickly. Danielle and I both know the only reason they made the two-hour drive from Chicago to Eastwood was to try to bust Danielle's lie.

Joke's on you, bitch.

"Are you going to see Grandpa?" Danielle asks, and I know

what she's thinking. Though, her grandpa would probably go along with this. He'd find it amusing, actually.

"Is he home? We could stop by on our way out of town."

"He might be." Danielle fidgets in her seat.

"Where else would the guy be?" Peter laughs. "He's retired, right? Pushing ninety. Of course he's home watching Jeopardy or something."

"It's Monday evening," I say, trying not to smile by the way Danielle is staring daggers at Peter. "He's at church."

"Right." Danielle nods. "He's volunteering tonight."

I wiggle my eyebrows. "That's just what he wants you to think. Did you forget about the church ladies?"

Danielle laughs and pulls her hand out of mine only to playfully push me away. "Oh my God, no. Stop it right now."

"Most of them are widowed, you know," I go on, laughing as well.

"Then I guess we should head out of town," Peter says.

Danielle raises her eyebrows. "So, you're not even going to say hi to Grandpa?"

Diana flicks her eyes to Peter. I can tell she wants to see her grandpa but won't risk disagreeing with this fucker. "He's busy." Diana shakes her head. "I don't want to bother him at church."

"What, are you afraid you'll get struck down by lightning if you try to enter the church or something?" Danielle says.

"There's a good chance I will be," Peter says, thinking he's being funny or smug or something. I really can't stand the guy and I've only been in his presence a few minutes.

"Well, we need to get back to work," I start. We really do, and I know Danielle wants to get away from her sister. "Did you still want that drink?" I ask Peter.

"Why not?" He grabs a menu from the center of the table. Danielle and I go back to work, and right as Danielle sets the food on her sister's table, Quinn and Scarlet walk in.

"Hey," I say to them as they take a seat at the bar. "You taking a night off from mommy-duty or something?"

"Mom has both kids," Quinn says, taking her purse off her shoulder and setting it on the bar top. "Archer got called in for emergency surgery and Wes is out tonight too. So we're being party animals and came in to order cheese fries and onion rings."

"I'll put your order in." Before I do, I look at Danielle, who's standing by her sister's table. Quinn follows my line of sight.

"Does Danielle know that couple?" she asks.

"Yeah. It's her sister and her fiancé."

Scarlet tips her head, blonde hair falling over her shoulder. "He looks like the kind of guy I used to hustle. He's got *douchebag wanting to prove he's hot shit* written all over him. AKA an easy target." She shrugs and turns back around in her barstool. "I thought her family lived on the coast."

"They do. They came for a surprise visit."

"Poor Danielle."

"You can say that again." I go into the kitchen, putting in the order for fries and onion rings. I fill a few drinks, clean up a couple tables, and wipe down the bar. Scarlet must have gotten up to use the bathroom or something, because Quinn is sitting alone at the bar, looking down at her phone.

I go over, resting my elbows on the wooden countertop.

"Could a fake diamond pass for a real engagement ring?"

Quinn looks up. eyes wide. "Are you proposing?"

"No."

"Way to get my hopes up."

I arch my eyebrows. "Asking about fake rings got your hopes up? Have a little higher expectations for me, sis."

"Fine. Sorry. And I suppose so. Why do you want to know?"

"Danielle's sister, Diana, is getting married in Hawaii soon, and I'm going with to pretend to be Danielle's fake fiancé."

"Logan," Quinn says but trails off, shaking her head. She doesn't have to say it for me to know what she's thinking. This is a terrible idea. "Can I at least know why you're posing as her fiancé?"

"She didn't want to go alone, and they wouldn't let her bring someone unless it *was serious*. Like engaged."

"That seems a little strict."

I nod, flicking my gaze to Diana and Peter. "They're not the best people, and this wedding is going to be awkward for Danielle. Her sister's fiancé made a move on Danielle about a year ago, and she got blamed for it because her dress was too short."

"Oh, hell no." Quinn shakes her head, instantly angered, and jerks around to glare at Peter. She shudders and turns back to me. "It doesn't matter if she was naked. If her sister's fiancé hit on her, it's his fault."

"Exactly. Like I said…not the best people. They run 5Ks on Thanksgiving."

Quinn gasps. "They're the worst."

"I know, right?"

"I have a ring that might work. The side stones are real diamonds but the big fat center one is cubic zirconia. I got it with the intention of swapping out the big stone with a sapphire, but then I realized it passed as real and kept creepers away at bars. I kind of forgot about it, but I'm pretty sure it's still upstairs in my jewelry box. I'll put it in the mailbox, and you can grab it on your way home tonight. Logan?" she asks, looking into my eyes. "Are you sure you want to do this?"

She won't say it, but she knows. She knows I have real feelings for Danielle. Real feeling I'm going to have to convince Danielle are only fake.

CHAPTER 9

LOGAN

"So you're telling me that I'm going to be down two bartenders?" Owen looks up from the plate of leftovers he brought home from Mom and Dad's.

I stare at him for a good few seconds. "That's all you're taking away from this?"

He shrugs. "Yeah. Now I have to work."

"Wow. What a crazy concept to *work* when you're at *work*." I take a seat at the kitchen table and pull a roll off Owen's plate. The fucker ate the rest while I was at work. "You did hear me, right?"

"Of course I heard you." Owen sits back, looking right at me. "You know I love you," he starts. "And I know you're in love with Danielle, even if you're not willing to admit it to anyone."

"I'm not—"

"Lie to yourself all you want." Owen picks up his fork. "But it's useless lying to me. I'm the better version of you, remember? I know everything."

I let out a slow breath and go to the fridge to get the second plate Mom sent over. Well, that's if Owen didn't eat it too. This is one of the rare occurrences where Owen is one hundred percent right. I like Danielle. I want to be more than friends with her, and I'm sure it is obvious.

"How long are you going to be gone?" Owen asks.

"We're leaving Thursday morning and will catch a late plane Sunday Hawaii time. I'm not sure when we'll get back here."

He sighs dramatically. "That's a whole weekend fucking gone."

I peel the foil off my plate and stick it in the microwave. "Working four days in a row won't kill you. Then again, I don't think you've ever worked four days in a row before. Now I'm questioning if you'll survive."

"Fucker."

I laugh and go to the pantry, grabbing treats for Dexter, who's been silently begging under the table this whole time.

"But the serious question is, can I trust you to take care of Dex, or do I need to drop him off with Mom?"

"Drop him off with Mom and you might not get him back."

"True," I say, holding out the treats. Dex plods over, tail wagging like crazy. "And you're too energetic for old Rufus."

"I can handle the dog. You know chicks love guys with a puppy anyway. He'll be my wingman since you're deserting me."

Owen and I have spent time apart, of course, but for most of our lives, we've done things together. Having a twin is like having a built-in best friend, and we get each other without even trying. Which isn't always a good thing. There are many things about Owen I'd rather *not* get.

"I'll call in and check on you every day," I tease. "Should I prepare meals for you too? Label them in the fridge with which day of the week you can eat them on?"

"You might have to. I'll run out of food on day one."

We both laugh, and I grab my food from the microwave and then join Owen at the table.

"But really," he goes on, tone changing. "This has to be it. You either make your move in Hawaii, finally tell her how you feel and do something about it…or you need to move on. I can't watch you spend the rest of your life on the sideline, just waiting for the ref to call you in. You need to put yourself in the game."

I push my food around on my plate, mind drifting to Danielle. Letting out a breath, I look up at Owen. He's right again, dammit.

"Regretting something you did sucks ass, trust me, I know," he goes on. "But regretting what you didn't do sucks even worse. Then you get stuck in the *what if* game and even I can lose sleep over that."

Shoveling a forkful of food into my mouth, I just nod. He's referencing his own personal regrets when it comes to love. His ex-girlfriend Charlotte still has his heart, and we found out last year she moved to New York and got engaged to some big shot lawyer. Owen took the news harder than anyone—including me —expected. He's still in love with her, even after all this time.

It kills me to see him hurting over her. They broke up because Owen was, well, Owen. Charlie wanted something more serious after college and Owen wasn't ready to settle down. Really, he was scared. We were young, just graduated, and didn't know what the hell we were supposed to do with our lives. Charlie was in law school, set on getting a job at her dad's firm here in Eastwood.

The thought of settling down, of being the second one out of all of us to get married and pop out babies…it freaked Owen out. I don't think he's even admitted it to himself, but I think he was more afraid of letting Charlie down than anything else.

So they broke up and she moved on, getting a fancy job in the city. That was years ago, and it still haunts him. I don't want to end up in the same situation with Danielle. I can't imagine watching her date anyone else. Fall in love with anyone else.

Marry anyone else.

I swallow my food and reach for my water. Owen is right: this has to be it. Because if this isn't…then it won't happen at all.

~

"I FUCKING HATE ALL OF YOU." I SET THE WEIGHTS DOWN AND glare at Owen, Dean, and Archer. It doesn't always happen that we end up at the gym at the same time, but when we do, we spend more time heckling each other than working out.

And right now, they won't shut the fuck up about Hawaii and what I should do to Danielle when we get there.

"If you need some pointers, I'm willing to share a few tips." Dean adds weights to the leg press.

"Don't take advice from him," Owen says. "He's married. And we all know what happens to your sex life when you get married. It disappears."

"I disagree," Archer starts, and we all round on him. Dean acts like he's going to puke, and Archer rolls his eyes. Archer is married to our baby sister. It's an unspoken rule he's not allowed to bring anything up that makes us think their relationship is more than PG. Even though they have one kid and are trying for another.

"Notice Dean didn't object," Owen laughs. "Proof that *most* married couples become boring."

"So what then?" Archer asks. "You'd just date forever and not get married and settle down?"

"That's the plan." Owen shrugs, turning away and picking up another weight. "It's worked well for me so far. And settling for just one pussy for the rest of your life? No thank you."

I don't bring up what he told me just last night and how I know he'd give anything for another chance with Charlie. For the next five minutes or so, we all lift and stop talking to each other. And then things pick right back up as we rest between reps.

"You really think you can pull this off?" Dean asks, stretching out his hamstrings.

"I don't see why it won't," I tell him, pulling one arm across my chest. "Her sister already bought it, and that ring I borrowed from Quinn looks legitimate."

"But then what?"

I shake my head. "I don't know. We go back to how things were."

"No, dude," Owen says firmly as he checks himself out in the large mirror. "You're going to fuck her so good she'll be begging for more."

I roll my eyes. "And I wonder why you're single."

"Whatever happens," Dean goes on, "enjoy the time off in paradise."

"I plan on it." Going anywhere with Danielle would feel like paradise. We go back to lifting and then finish our workout. Archer and Dean go their separate ways, and Owen and I stop into town to grocery shop and run a few other errands before we head home as well.

Ever since we opened Getaway, we knew we'd be working our asses off until it took off enough to hire more employees so we could take more days off ourselves. We're definitely to that point but still work like we did when we were new. Well, I do at least. Owen shows up, complains about having to work, but doesn't mind as much as he makes you believe. He's working tonight, and I have the night off before going back tomorrow. Maybe we should hire another bartender or two as well as a few weekend waitresses.

I plan on spending the rest of the day finishing the thriller I started—I'm only five chapters away from the end and shit's about to go down—and then take Dex for a walk. I'm on my last chapter when Danielle texts me.

It's info on the hotel we're staying at, along with the flight numbers. We have two layovers, but we're lucky enough that we were able to get any tickets this close to the wedding. I click on the hotel link.

"Shit," I mutter. This place is fancy, and the beaches are endless. It really does look like a paradise.

Just a minute later, my phone rings, and it's Danielle.

"Miss me?" I answer.

"You know it, Dawson," she says right back. "I assume you got the hotel info."

"I was looking at it and then someone had the nerve to call and interrupt me."

"Geez, that person sounds like a jerk."

"The biggest."

"Other than being rudely interrupted, what are you doing?" she asks.

"Trying to finish a book."

"How close to the end are you?"

I flip through it. "Twenty pages."

"That'll take you like ten minutes," she laughs. "Want to finish it and then come over? I made a bunch of pies and need someone to help me eat them."

"Pies?"

"I got suckered into a charity bake sale for the 4H group. I've never made a pie before, but my grandma was the best pie baker in the county. Or at least Grandpa says so. Now I have to live up to the expectation she set."

"Eating dessert in the name of charity? That's basically torture."

"I know, right? And I'm about to make a fresh pot of coffee to go along with it."

"Damn, you're evil. I'll be right over," I chuckle. "But I'm finishing the book first."

"Thanks. And that'll be perfect timing. I have two more pies in the oven."

"How many pies did you make?"

She pauses as she counts. "Eight."

"Who the fuck has eight pie-pans?"

A giggle comes over the phone, and it's one of the best sounds in the whole damn world. "I love how that's your main concern. We have five pie-pans, and then I went out and got those cheap ones. I was going to make every pie in my grandma's recipe book, but I'm eight in and there's still two more pages of recipes. I didn't know this until this morning, but she always wanted to open a bakery. Grandpa told me she spent years saving up the money and found the perfect location and everything. Then she got sick," Danielle says, voice thinning. Danielle's grandma died before she got the chance to meet her.

"What was the perfect location?"

"Downtown, where that overpriced boutique is now."

"Pies would sell better than expensive clothes. This is Eastwood, not Newport. We're not sophisticated enough to follow trends. I mean, if it's plaid and pairs well with John Deer green, you've hit most of your market in this town."

Danielle laughs again, and it hits me then how far I'd go to make her smile and hear her laugh. It hurts me to know she's hurting.

Motherfucker. I'm so screwed. Because no matter how I go about this, there is no possible way I can deny that I am crazy in love with this woman.

CHAPTER 10

DANIELLE

"I made that lasagna you like and put it in the freezer. And the award-winning pie is in the cake stand on the counter." I go over to the fridge, making sure it's well stocked before I leave for the airport.

"Kiddo," Grandpa says, limping a bit as he walks through the kitchen. "I know where the grocery store is. And even better, I know how to order a pizza."

"But they don't deliver out here," I counter.

"I have the truck."

I put one hand on my hip. "I know. I just…I feel bad leaving."

Grandpa laughs. "I have enjoyed having you here. It's nice having the company, and it was high time someone got out Grandma's cookbook." He eyes the pie on the counter.

"Don't eat it all in one day," I say with a laugh.

Grandpa gives me a wink. "I'll try my best."

Black Cat jumps up on the counter and sniffs at the glass cake stand. Good thing I covered the pie. The porch creaks, and a second later, someone knocks on the door. My heart swells in my chest—just a tiny bit—knowing that Logan is here.

"I'll miss you," I tell Grandpa before I go to answer the door. "Take care while I'm gone, okay?"

"I've gotten along this far and have been just fine. Now *you* take care. Let me know when you land. And watch out for sharks," he adds, knowing I have a very real fear of wildlife in the ocean.

I shudder. "I'll be staying in knee-deep water."

"The shallow end is no place to live, kiddo. Go out there. Get your hair wet."

"You're not just talking about the ocean anymore, are you?"

Grandpa just shrugs and limps past me to let Logan and Dean —who's driving us to the airport—into the house. I'm surprised to see Kara there with them. She smiles when she sees me, and I have to give her credit for trying. She's the odd one out with the Dawsons, and her little stint where she was mad at Quinn for being pregnant at her wedding left a sour taste in their mouths.

The Dawson guys are very protective of their little sister, and anyone—even Dean's wife—being mean to her puts you on their shit list. Add in that her anger was directed toward Quinn *and* Archer, who's just as much of a Dawson as the rest of them, and Logan and Owen were not her biggest fan.

"Hey, you're coming with?" I ask, hoping I don't come off as rude.

"Yeah, we figured since we're dropping you off at the airport around dinner time, we might as well take advantage of it and have dinner in the city," she explains.

"Ohhh, that sounds fun." I look at Logan, and this time there's no denying the beat my heart skipped. "My suitcase is over there. It's heavy."

Logan raises an eyebrow. "Bummer, you're going to have to deal with a heavy suitcase."

I laugh right as he steps forward to get it for me. I double-check I have our boarding passes and then the other stuff I need before leaving for a few days.

"Take care of my granddaughter," Grandpa tells Logan, clapping him on the back. "Have fun, and don't do anything I wouldn't do."

Logan gives me a look, and I narrow my eyes, shaking my head in a silent warning not to make a comment about church ladies again.

"We'll have fun," I say. "And then we'll suffer through Diana's wedding."

"Have a drink or two first." Grandpa winks, and Dean laughs. The day after Diana and Peter left Eastwood, she's become an insufferable Bridezilla and went so far as "advising" me I should cut my hair before the wedding since Hawaii is so hot. Turns out, she wants to have the longest hair out of everyone in the bridal party. I did go get a haircut but got exactly one inch taken off only to clean up my split ends.

I'm not allowed to wear my hair down during the ceremony or have on dangly earrings. We also can't have red lipstick, because that's Diana's "signature" color. She also wants us all to fast the day before the wedding to make sure we "look our best" and not bloated in the wedding photos.

I'm starting to think she and Peter deserve each other.

"Send me pictures," Grandpa says, hobbling over.

"I will. Love you, Grandpa."

"Love you too, Ellie."

I give him a hug goodbye and then step into the humid summer air. Logan puts my suitcase in the trunk, and we climb into the back of Dean's car.

~

"We have an hour and a half before we leave." Logan looks around the terminal. "Want to go get something to eat?"

"Yeah, that sounds good. I'm starving." I grab my purse and reach for my carry-on, but Logan grabs it first, along with his.

Carrying both bags, Logan leads the way, stopping outside a pizza restaurant. He looks at it and shrugs. I nod and we go in, finding a table. Logan stashes the bags to the side, and we order drinks and a pepperoni pizza.

"What's the first thing you want to do when we get to Hawaii?" I ask, reaching for my Long Island Iced Tea.

"Sleep."

"You're so boring."

Logan takes a sip of beer. "It'll be six AM our time and one AM Hawaii time. I can't sleep on planes, but that might work to my advantage. I can pass out once we get to the hotel and then wake up and be pretty much on their time zone."

"I can sleep on long flights if I'm tired enough."

"Right. You've been on some long ones."

Nodding, I turn my head, people watching for a minute. I turn back, and Logan quickly looks away. I smile and run my eyes over him. God, he's such a gorgeous man. He's been working out a lot more lately, and I can tell. It won't be hard to pretend to be insanely attracted to my fiancé.

What the hell did I get us into?

"Thanks again for coming with me," I blurt before I have a chance to really think about it. I reach out and put my hand on his, and as soon as my skin makes contact with his, I know I just make a big mistake.

Because now I'm not entirely sure I'm going to be capable of removing my hand.

His long fingers under mine are warm, and I know if he was to flip his palm over, I'd feel rough skin. He'd interlace our fingers, and he'd move his thumb down to my wrist, rubbing little circles over my skin.

Then he'd reach forward with his other hand and caress my face. We'd slowly lean across the table. He'd push my hair back, tucking my long locks behind my ear. My tongue would dart out, slowly wetting my lips. Heat would rush through me, starting in my stomach and spreading down at a scary-fast rate, making me wet with anticipation of what's to come.

Spoiler alert: it'll be me.

I blink and jerk my hand back, unable to help that flush that takes over my face. Reaching for my drink, I almost knock it over before I grip the cold glass. I bring it to my lips and take down a few gulps, which was probably a bad idea on its own. I haven't eaten in a while, the pizza won't be here for another ten minutes at least, and drunk Danielle has an even harder time filtering her thoughts.

"You're welcome," Logan says, leaning back and tensing a bit. "I know how awkward it would be around your family, and I'm glad you don't have to go alone." The line sounds rehearsed, but I'll take it.

"Yeah. I've hardly spoken to my dad since I left. Which is a good thing, because it was really awkward when he called to congratulate me on my engagement," I laugh, and Logan does too. I shake my head. "I still feel bad for getting you into this mess."

"It's really not that messy." Logan's shoulders start to relax again. "And if I didn't want to get into it, I wouldn't. I know this might come as a shock since I spend most of my free time with Owen, but I am an adult capable of making my own decisions."

I narrow my eyes. "But are you really?"

"It is a little questionable. You should start making me precooked dinners and pies when we get back like you did for your grandpa."

"Hey," I laugh. "Grandpa has gotten used to having someone else around the house to help with those things. His age is starting to show, as much as I hate saying that. And it's a wonder his cholesterol isn't sky-high from the way he was eating before I got there."

"You mean eating the burgers and fries he'd come in and get at least four times a week?"

"Exactly that." I pick up my drink again. "Now I'm the one eating burgers and fries four times a week."

"They are good burgers."

"Too good. I should have scaled back before summer and swimsuit weather."

Logan looks at me like I'm crazy. "You're kidding, right?"

I make a face, getting a little uncomfortable. I spoke without thinking, and to be honest, I'm not even sure I care that much. But it's been so ingrained in my head since I was just a little girl that how I look determines my self-worth in some peoples' eyes.

It's utter bullshit, and I know it. Yet I have a hard time turning that part of my brain off, the part where I look at myself in the mirror and immediately see my flaws. They're the first things I see, actually.

I'd love to look at myself and find beauty in the imperfections, but I don't know how.

"You look really good in a swimsuit," Logan says, and now it's his turn to speak without thinking. "I mean, not that I really look or anything."

The alcohol is hitting me and watching him blush is the cutest thing in the whole entire world right now. "You've never looked at me in a swimsuit?" I flutter my lashes.

Logan shakes his head, recovering fast. "Nope. I refuse to look at you when you're indecent." He brings his beer to his lips.

I lean forward and bite my lip. "So you're not going to go to the beach with me at all this weekend?"

"Only if you wear one of those old-fashioned swimsuits."

"Like the one Wednesday Addams wore in *Family Values*?"

Logan laughs, eyes sparkling. "Exactly like that one."

The pizza comes, and after we eat, we walk around the airport, not wanting to sit when we have an eight-hour flight ahead of us. We're in a little gift shop that has the most random crap. There's a little display of bumper stickers, and I grab one that would be perfect for Owen's car.

"I make frequent stops at your mom's house," Logan reads, looking over my shoulder. "I'm getting it."

"Any bets on how long it'll take him to notice this time?"

"Hopefully more than a day."

I laugh. "You had that last one on your car for a week."

Logan shakes his head. "I've gotten in the habit of circling my car at least once a day to check." He and Owen have a long-running prank of putting stupid or sometimes straight-out offensive bumper stickers on each other's cars and then seeing how it takes to notice.

We walk through the airport some more and then go back to the terminal right in time to line up to board. We head to the back of the plane and take our seats. I spend a few minutes arranging my stuff and pulling out my blanket from my bag.

"Oh, I almost forgot." I get the ring out of my wallet. The center stone isn't a real diamond, but the side stones are, and I really am a little worried about losing it. How do people wear expensive engagement rings so casually?

I slip the ring on and hold up my hand, wiggling my fingers. I turn, expecting to see Logan smiling or rolling his eyes. But he has a look of disappointment on his face, and that bad feeling starts to rise in my stomach again.

Did I make a huge mistake—again?

Logan is my best friend, and he's going to pretend to be deeply in love and excited to marry me. It's all fun and games for now. But what's going to happen when we come back to Eastwood?

CHAPTER 11

DANIELLE

I carefully pull Logan's earbuds out of his ears and take the iPad from his lap, shutting it off and putting it away in his carry-on bag. The pilot just came on and asked us all to turn off our electronic devices so we can start our descent. It's been rather cold this whole flight, and Logan and I were sharing my blanket as we watched *Infinity War* together on the iPad. Logan fell asleep halfway through, and I'm feeling just as sleepy.

After putting my own stuff away, I buckle my seat belt and look at Logan's lap, biting my lip. I don't know if his seatbelt is on, thanks to the blanket. I lift it up so I can check. His seat belt isn't buckled, and I don't want to wake him up. Unbuckling mine again, I lean over, trying to find both parts to his seatbelt so I can click it into place.

I can't reach it, so I drop to my knees and inch closer. And then the plane hits a bit of turbulence. I pitch forward, hitting my forehead on Logan's knee.

"Trying to cop a feel?" he asks, looking at me quizzically.

"Oh, you'd know if I was trying, because I would have succeeded." I put one hand on his leg and push myself up. "I was trying to put your seat belt on. We're going to land soon."

"Told you I wasn't a fully functional adult." He smiles and runs his hand through his hair, messing it up. "Can't even put my own seatbelt on."

"Ha-ha. You so do believe that's all I was trying to do. For all you know I could have been trying to steal your wallet. Maybe this whole thing was a ruse to get you to come to Hawaii with me so I could start a new life of crime."

He reaches down and clicks the seatbelt into place. "And this is coming from the person who thought washing dirty money meant actually washing dollar bills with soap and water."

"It's a very misleading expression."

"Just like the steak-fries," he says with a snort of laughter.

I narrow my eyes and put my seatbelt back on. "It's an honest mistake and one I really think you should let go."

"No way. I'm forever going to be reminding you of the time you asked for 'regular fries' because you really didn't want strips of steak along with your burger."

"That's a lot of meat!" I laugh. "And I thought you said you don't fall asleep on planes."

"I never have before. You bored me to sleep."

"Jerk."

The plane hits another patch of turbulence, startling me. I reach down for the armrest, forgetting we put it up. My hand comes down on Logan's thigh, but I don't take it off. The plane continues to bump along, and my mind flashes to seeing the oxygen masks coming down and everyone screaming as the plane plummets into the ocean.

"It's okay." Logan puts his hand on top of mine, and his touch is comforting. "Just a bit of turbulence."

"A bit?" I press my hand against his thigh to keep me from flipping mine over and slipping my fingers through his. Though gripping his thigh isn't much better. I let out a slow breath. "I'm not really a nervous flyer, but there's something about being over the ocean that freaks me out."

Logan looks out the window at the dark ocean. "I think we'd have a better chance of surviving a crash into water than on land."

"Only to drown and get eaten by a megalodon."

"Those aren't real."

"They might be. There's so much stuff in the ocean we haven't discovered yet."

The plane bumps again, and I press my head against the headrest. Logan curls his fingers around my palm.

"Is this your first time visiting Hawaii?" the woman next to me asks.

"Yeah," I tell her. "You?"

"Oh no, this is our fourth trip." She motions to another woman who's sitting a row ahead of us. "We just love it here." Her eyes fall to Logan's hand on mine. "There's so much to do we come back every year to try and check another thing off our list."

"I was really hoping to do the Road to Hana, but I don't think we'll have time before the wedding."

A broad smile breaks out on the woman's face. "You're getting married?"

"My sister is."

She looks at my left hand, eyeing the engagement ring. "You'll be planning your wedding here next."

I laugh. "I don't know about that."

She looks past me at Logan. "You're a lucky man."

Logan turns his head toward mine, smiling. We don't even know this woman. It's a good test on our plan to be fake-engaged.

"Yeah." He squeezes my hand. "I am."

"Have you started planning your wedding yet?"

"No, not yet," he answers.

"Good," the woman laughs. "Because seeing one Hawaiian wedding is enough to make you want to get married on the beach as well."

"I'm sure it'll be amazing," Logan says. "But I think something a little more laid back is more our style, right babe?"

"Yeah. Something a little more country. I do like the idea of an outdoor ceremony, with the reception in a big, old barn."

"Oh, those rustic weddings are trendy," the woman says.

"We wouldn't do it for the trend," Logan tells her. "It just fits us."

And now I know pretending to be a couple is wrong. But dammit, this type of wrong feels so fucking good.

~

"Wow." Everything is dark, but the view is still incredible. A slight breeze rustles my hair, and I grip the balcony railing, looking out at the beach and ocean. "It's so beautiful."

"Yeah, it is." Logan steps next to me, resting his elbows on the railing as he looks out. "It's quieter than I thought it would be."

"It's like two AM."

"And seven AM for us. I think I'm at the point of being so tired I'm not tired anymore."

"You napped on the plane." I tip my head toward him, nudging him with my hip. It's something I've done before, but for some reason, the contact feels too intimate. "I'm tired, but the thought of changing into my PJs, washing my face, and brushing my teeth seems too daunting. So I'm going to stand here being tired and not doing anything about it."

"Smart, Danielle."

"You don't know the struggle of wanting to crash but having to take off makeup."

"Can't you just sleep in it for one night?"

"It's bad for your skin, plus I'll wake up with eyeliner and mascara smeared all over my face."

Logan chuckles softly. "That would be a scary sight."

"Terrifying. Just wait until you see me with bed head too."

The muscles in Logan's jaw tense and he pushes off the balcony, looking at me with what I can only describe as confusion on his face, as if he doesn't know what to think or how to act right now.

Neither do I.

"You really should go to bed."

"Yeah," I breathe and take another look out at the dark ocean before following Logan into the room. He uses the bathroom and showers while I unpack my suitcase. I pile my hair into a tight bun on the top of my head and sit on the bed, waiting for my turn to shower.

Logan comes out of the bathroom wearing grey sweatpants. His hair is damp, and his skin is reddened from the hot water. He's holding his towel and brings it up to his head, rubbing it over his hair once more.

Everything inside me feels all squishy, and I instantly regret not packing my vibrator. Not like I could use it, though.

"H-how was your shower?" I fumble over my words, mentally yelling at myself to stop staring at Logan. My eyes are on his muscular chest right now, and when I try to look away, my gaze drops to his crotch. There's a bulge in his pants, and when he takes a step closer to the bed, I can see the outline of his large dick.

I squeeze my eyes closed and reach up to play with my hair like I do when I'm nervous, forgetting that I have it in a ridiculous topknot. Why the hell does Logan have to be so damn attractive? It's downright rude of him to be so tan and fit, sporting the perfect five o'clock shadow. And the *nerve* of him to wear gray fucking sweatpants. The only thing worse would be him coming out in a well-tailored suit, which he's going to be wearing Saturday for the wedding.

I.

Am.

So.

Fucked.

"It was fine." He hangs up the towel and looks at me on the bed. "So…how is this going to work?"

I pull the band out of my hair, needing something to do with my hands that's *not* running them over every ripple of muscle on Logan's body.

"How is…is what going to work?"

"Sleeping. There's only one bed. And two of us."

"Oh, right." I blink and let out a breath. "It's a big bed."

"Plenty of room for us both?" Logan raises an eyebrow. "I don't want to make you uncomfortable. I can sleep on the couch."

"That's not a couch." I wave my hand at the little love seat near the balcony door. "You stay on one side and I stay on the other, and we'll be fine. And don't get handsy."

He gives me a cheeky grin.

Dammit, Logan. Stop being so adorable and sexy at the same time.

"I can't make any promises."

My eyes go to his hands. His large hands with long fingers and rough skin on his palms. Hands that would feel so good on my body. Spreading my legs. Slowly moving between my thighs and up to my—

"I'm going to get in the shower." I almost fall off the bed I get up so fast. I grab my stuff and buzz past him and into the bathroom, leaning against the door as soon as I get it closed. My heart is hammering in my chest, and it feels like I'm doing something wrong again.

But am I?

Shaking myself, I put my hair back into a bun and start the shower. The water is warm and feels so good rushing down on my skin. I should lower the temperature and stand here shivering the desire right off me, because my body is craving it bad right now.

Turning my thoughts to something much less pleasant, I sit

on the shower floor to shave my legs and think about seeing my family in the morning. It's sad, really, how strained things are between me and my parents. Growing up, I used to think I must have been adopted since I was so different than the rest of my family.

Feeling like you don't fit in with your own family is an isolating feeling, one I can't really explain. I wanted to fit in. I wanted to make my parents proud. So for years, I did what I thought I was supposed to do. I followed Dad's "ten-year plan" only to get toward the end of that ten years and look back and mourn the wasted time.

I can't change the past, and regrets only rob me from any happiness the present can offer. But I do wonder what life would have been like if I had done what I wanted to do instead of what was expected of me. Maybe I'd feel like I knew who I was, and I'd have a purpose in this world.

Or maybe not.

Maybe I'm damned to always feel like this. Never really fitting in anywhere. Not really having a sense of identity. Not having anything that truly defines me.

I swallow the lump that's rising in my throat and think about Logan. And then the reason why I'm so scared to be more than friends hits me like a punch to the gut.

How can I expect anyone to love me when I don't even know who I am?

CHAPTER 12

LOGAN

I pull the curtains closed, blocking out the light, and get back into bed. Danielle is sound asleep, and waking up with her next to me brought up a feeling inside me that I can't quite figure out.

It feels right.

But it's wrong.

We're pretending.

I want this to be real.

And the more we fake it, the more we put on the masks of happy lovers, the more it feels like it's not going to really happen. Doesn't quite make sense, I know.

Luckily, Danielle took a long shower last night and I fell asleep before she got into bed. If I'd still been awake, I don't know if I would have been able to sleep knowing that next to me, only an arm's length apart, was the woman I've been in love with since the moment I met her.

It's early in the morning, but the sun is already up and shining brightly down on the beach right outside our window. I actually have no idea what we're supposed to do today, but I know at some point we're having breakfast or brunch—or lunch at this point—with Danielle's parents.

I stick my legs back under the covers, and Danielle rolls over. She sleeps on her back, with one hand up on the pillow above her head. Her long hair is a tangled mess around her face, and one of the straps of her tank top fell down over her shoulder. With no makeup and no bra, she's even more gorgeous than when she's done herself all up.

My eyelids get heavy, and I start to drift back to sleep. Then Danielle's phone rings. It's on silent and buzzes on the nightstand next to her. She doesn't so much as stir. I push up and reach over to grab the phone. It's her mom calling, and I silence it, not seeing the point in waking her up yet.

Unless we were supposed to go to breakfast with them. Oh well. I set the phone back down and close my eyes again. About ten minutes later, someone knocks on the door. This time, Danielle wakes up. She's facing me, and her eyes go to me as soon as they open.

"Hey," she says, voice thick with sleep. "Was someone knocking, or did I dream that?"

"Someone is knocking." I get out of bed, adjusting my pants as I stride to the door and look through the peephole. "It's your sister and two other people," I say to Danielle. "Want me to let them in?"

"Yeah. There's no need to delay the inevitable any longer than necessary." She sits up, pushing her long hair out of her face before getting out of bed. She's wearing pink sleeper shorts and a white tank top that ends right above her belly button. I'm sure she wears that most nights. It's far from lingerie and looks quite comfortable.

But, fuck me, she looks good in it. The shorts ride up on her ass as she crosses the room, and if her hair wasn't hanging over her breasts, I'm sure I'd be able to see her nipples through the thin white tank top.

It's like she did it on purpose to drive me crazy. It's cruel, really, to have her flaunting that body around when I can't have it. And to think she was next to me all night...now I'm really fucking glad I fell asleep before I saw her get into bed looking like that.

I swallow hard, tearing my eyes away from her, and look back at the door. I'm already insanely attracted to her. The last thing I need is to get a hard-on right before I welcome her sister and presumably her mother into our room.

Though it would help our fake couple story to have it look like they interrupted morning sex. I undo the chain on the door and open it. All three women on the other side of the door widen their eyes and look me up and down.

"Hey," I say to Diana as Danielle appears beside me. The older woman next to Diana looks from me to Danielle and smiles.

"Hi, Mom."

The woman steps forward, pulling Danielle into a tight hug that lasts exactly two seconds. Everyone shuffles into the room. "This must be Logan, your fiancé."

Danielle tips her head to me, smiling, and I wrap my arm around her shoulders. "Yeah, it is. Logan, this is my mom and..." she trails off, looking at the other woman.

"Nancy," she introduces herself. "Mother of the groom."

"It's nice to meet you," I say and extend my other hand. "And you too, Mrs. Cross."

Danielle's mom laughs, high-pitched and fake. "Please, call me Carol. We're going to be family soon enough. Have you two talked about wedding dates yet?"

Diana looks annoyed at the mention of Danielle's wedding, reminding me of another family member who was a huge bitch around her wedding as well.

"Not yet." Danielle waves her hand in the air, not meaning to flash the big—fake—ring through the air. She looks at me again, eyes shining. "We're in no rush and really, this is Diana's weekend. That's why I didn't announce anything on social media yet."

"Then why didn't you just wait to ask her?" Diana smiles sweetly. "I can't imagine not shouting it from the rooftops the moment I got engaged."

Danielle's shoulders bunch up, and she laughs nervously, eyes going to me.

"It wasn't about letting the world know," I start before she has a chance to start rambling. I run my fingers down Danielle's arm, and my heart speeds up. Angling my body toward hers, I reach out with my other hand and push her messy hair over her shoulder. "It was about not being able to wait another day to let Danielle know how much she means to me."

The words come out easily but leave a bad taste in my mouth. I'm acting, yet I'm not, and the weird disassociation from the truth is enough to make me dizzy.

"I had a whole big thing planned," I go on. "I was going to ask during our town's annual Fourth of July fireworks show. But like I said, I got impatient. I knew from the moment she walked into my bar at one AM on a Thursday that she was perfect for me." I let my hand drop, and I take both her hands in mine, getting lost in her sea-green eyes. She gives my hands a squeeze and blinks rapidly, almost as if she's trying not to cry.

I don't know if she's acting or not.

"Oh, how romantic," Peter's mother swoons. "And how thoughtful of you two to keep the news to yourselves until after the wedding."

"I try." Danielle nervously laughs. I lace my fingers through hers and give her hands a squeeze. She has nothing to be nervous about. I'll make sure we get through this. "Are you going down for breakfast already? I thought it was later."

"It is, but we were on our way down to get mimosas and get some sun before our reservation and thought we'd see if you'd like to join," her mother says. "I called."

"You did? We must have slept right through it."

"Up late?" Diana slightly narrows her eyes, and I can't tell if she's trying to be condescending or make a joke. There's a good chance not even she knows the difference between the two.

"We got in at like two or three AM. Yeah, we were up late."

"And then up a little later. I can't keep my hands off this one." I pull Danielle close to me, and her eyes widen as she tries not to laugh. Her mother looks at us disapprovingly and Diana's eyes narrow again.

"Try to keep it classy, Danielle. We'll be downstairs whenever you're ready. Don't be late to breakfast," her mother says. "It was nice to meet you, Logan. I look forward to getting to know you better before you become part of the family. Danielle's father does too."

They turn and filter out of the hotel room, shutting the door behind them.

"I can't keep my hands off this one?" Danielle hisses, shaking her head as she goes back to the bed. "Seriously?"

I shrug. "We're very much in love. Though really it would be the other way around." I turn to the mirror and flex the muscles in my chest. "I mean, look at me. How you're resisting me right now, I'll never know."

Danielle's cheeks flush, and she looks away. "I…I should get ready." She grabs her stuff and goes into the bathroom. I grab my phone and go onto the balcony, taking a few pictures to send to Owen so I can remind him that I'm here on a mini vacation while he's stuck at home working double shifts to fill in for Danielle and me. He responds right away.

Owen: You woke me up, cocksucker.

Me: Just "me"? You're alone tonight?

Owen: Fuck no. Wendy. Or Wanda? Hell if I know. Is still passed out. Did you fuck Danielle yet?

Me: How's Dexter? Did you remember to feed him?

Owen: You measured his food in baggies and left them on the counter. And labeled them for each day.

Me: Is that too hard for you?

Owen: Fuck you. And you didn't answer me. Did you put the P in the V??

Me: You need to grow the fuck up. And no.

Owen: Make me proud. Get out of the friendzone.

I lock the screen on my phone and set it down, looking out at the beach. It's early, but a lot of people are out there already.

"I'll do my makeup out here," Danielle says from inside the room. "So I'm not hogging the bathroom."

I get up and go back inside. "Wow." It's all I can do to keep my jaw from dropping. "You look beautiful."

Danielle wrinkles her nose and looks down at the dress. It's light pink, low-cut, and flows around her legs when she walks. "I don't look like I'm trying too hard to be on a tropical vacation?"

"You are on a tropical vacation."

She laughs. "Well, thanks. You better look good too, Dawson. I need to show off my arm candy."

I get my shit and go into the bathroom to get ready. I'm done before Danielle and take my book onto the balcony to read. Half an hour later, Danielle's hair is curled.

"This is why I don't curl my hair that often." She runs her fingers through it and looks in the mirror. "I have too much hair. Sometimes I consider chopping it all off."

"That'd make your sister happy."

She lets out a snort of laughter. "Right?"

I stick my phone and wallet in my pocket and lead the way out of the room. Neither of us talk as we walk down the hall and into the elevator. I take another look at Danielle once we get in, crowding to the back as another family pushes in with several large suitcases.

Danielle reaches up with her left hand, pushing her curls back and the ring gets stuck in her hair.

"Hang on," I tell her, angling my body toward hers and cupping my hand around her fingers. Danielle is wearing heels today like she usually does, but I'm still several inches taller than her. I look at the ring, seeing several strands of hair stuck under the little brackets that hold the fake diamond into place.

I move my gaze to her face…to her long lashes and her brilliantly bright eyes. And then to her lips that are parted and covered in dark pink lip gloss. If I look farther down, I'll see the swells of her breasts under her dress and will remember all too well how she looked this morning.

"Ow!" She winces, and I realize I just pulled her hair. Clearing my throat and forcing myself to focus on the task at hand, I carefully untangle her hair until she's free. "I'll try to remember not to do that again."

"Show off the ring and then take it off," I suggest. "Say you're worried you'll lose it on the beach or something."

"Good idea."

The elevator stops on the main lobby and everyone gets out. It takes us a while to figure out where to go since this place is fucking huge. I spot Danielle's mother and sister right as she comes to a dead stop.

"What's wrong?" I ask, turning and seeing her wringing her hands.

"It's the whole fucking bridal party."

"Yeah? They're here for the wedding."

She shakes her head. "I know…it's…it's just who's in it."

"Bad history?"

Her eyes close in a long blink. "Not really. It's just…it's stupid. I'm an adult and shouldn't worry about these things, right?"

"I don't want to agree or disagree until I know the full story."

Danielle lets out a breath. "I shouldn't care anymore. I…I don't want to care anymore. I'm a grown woman. I'm happy. I like my life in Eastwood, and while I would maybe go back and do a few things differently, I like to believe what Grandpa says. What happened yesterday is the reason for where I am today. Good or bad, you can't change the past." She nods. "You can only accept that all you have is your next choice. And I'm choosing not to give a fuck."

I tip my head, watching her wring her hands. "I think that was the start to a motivational speech, but I'm a little fucking confused."

Her eyes flutter shut, and she lets out a deep breath, trying hard to relax. What the hell is going on inside her head right now?

"Those girls have been my sister's friends for years. I know them, and they know me. And trust me when I say they make Regina George look like a saint."

"It's your fault I understand that reference."

Her lips curve into a small smile. "It's a good movie. I can't believe you'd never seen it before. But that's not the point. The point is, with that group of *plastics,* where you went to grad school and how many country clubs you've been to in the last year is all that matters."

"So, you're saying they're not going to be impressed with a bartender from Eastwood?" I rub my hands together. "I'm going to have fun with this."

More tension leaves Danielle's shoulders. "They'd be impressed if they knew how profitable Getaway was."

I shrug. "We don't do too bad for ourselves."

"Oh come on, Logan. I know I don't have access to the books, but I know you guys are bringing in a hell of a decent profit. Owen brings it up any time he's had a few shots and there's a pretty girl at the bar. Which is basically every night."

I let out a sigh and shake my head. "Sometimes I feel bad for getting all the smarts. It's like that thing where one twin absorbs the other started to happen and I got all the brains between the two of us."

Danielle laughs, and my own heart swells. "It is a little unfair. At least he has your looks, because those alone will get you far."

My jaw drops and I bring my hand to my chest. "Are you hitting on me, Danielle Cross?"

"You wish, Dawson." She playfully punches me and then slips her arm through mine. "Thank you, Logan."

"For what?"

She looks up at me. "You know."

CHAPTER 13

DANIELLE

"I'll have a mimosa," I tell the waiter. "But can I get vodka instead of champagne, and then hold the orange juice?"

The waiter lowers his notepad and blinks. "You just want vodka?"

"Yes." I close my drink menu. "Make it a double, please."

"Interesting way to start the day but a good choice nonetheless," he says with a chuckle. "And for you, sir?"

"I'll have the same but with the orange juice," Logan orders even though he hates vodka. He's a beer and whiskey drinker. Occasionally, he'll take a shot or two of tequila. But vodka…nope. He said he drank too much during college and it ruined it for him.

"You okay?" Logan asks when the waiter steps away. We're sitting at the end of a large table, surrounded by my sister's friends. Two have been her friend since high school, and she met the others during college.

"Physically, I'm fine. I even agree with you that this dress looks good on me. But mentally." I widen my eyes and make a face. "That's a whole different story."

Logan gives me a small smile, knowing me all too well. I can't distract him from the question at hand with my lame jokes. He sees right through it. I flick my eyes to my sister and her friends again, and it brings up a maelstrom of emotions too messy to even sort out in my head.

They are judgmental bitches who pick others apart in order to make themselves feel better, but that's not the only thing bugging me. I don't have a bunch of close girlfriends. I've never belonged to a group like that. I don't talk to anyone I went to high school with anymore, and while I'm Facebook friends with a few girls I hung out with in college, we never see each other in real life. We don't even message back and forth anymore, just occasionally like each other's photos.

I've told myself it's fine since I've always been a bit of a loner. I'm happy by myself, and even if I did have a big group of gal-pals that invited me out every other night, I'd probably turn the invites down.

So why does seeing my sister talk and laugh with her six best friends make my brain jump right to *there's something wrong with me* for not having a group of friends I can pose for photos with, posting them all over social media with cheesy captions about "my tribe" and how I couldn't get through life without them.

I'm sitting on solid ground, but it feels like the earth is crumbling out from under me. That weird sense of not knowing who I am creeps back up, and I feel the most unwelcome urge to try and fit in with these women, because I've been told over and over and over throughout my life that *not* being included is bad. I squeeze my eyes closed and try to quiet the sudden noise in my brain that's louder than the crashing wave on the shore.

"Danielle?" Logan's hand lands on mine. I open my eyes, and everything settles back into place. "What's going on?"

"Nothing, I just..." The waiter comes back with our drinks and then takes our breakfast order.

"You were saying?" Logan encourages.

I grab my drink and swirl the vodka around in the glass. And then I see someone else walking over. "Drink up," I tell Logan in a warning and bring my glass to my lips. The vodka doesn't go down as smooth as I anticipated, and I'm coughing and choking as my father and Peter's dad come to the table. Peter's father takes a seat and my own dad goes to Diana first, smiling down as he talks to her.

Then his eyes zero in on me. "Danielle," he says as he comes over.

"Hey, Dad." I stand up to give him a hug. I love my father, and I know he loves me. He really does want what's best for me, but we could never agree on what that was. He mapped everything out without consulting me, and not following through with his plans caused him to be disappointed in me.

"And this must be the young man you've told us nothing about." Dad looks at Logan, who stands and introduces himself. "You know," Dad starts after shaking Logan's hand, "Peter asked my permission before he proposed to Diana."

I press my lips together in a smile to keep from saying what I really feel about that. This is Diana's wedding weekend, bought and paid for. There's no changing her mind now and making a scene would just be bitchy.

"You two work together?" Dad asks.

"Yeah," I reply. "Logan owns the bar I work at."

"Glad that Yale education I paid for is going to good use," Dad laughs, but the joke falls flat…if you could consider that a joke at all.

"Danielle's amazing," Logan says quickly. "She already expanded the business and nearly doubled our sales."

"Sounds like she should be a partner in this little venture. Though once you're married, what's yours is hers and what's hers is yours. Though you have plenty of time to discuss that before the wedding."

"We will."

"Give me fair warning before I pay for another big wedding," Dad says with a laugh again.

"I don't want a big wedding," I say.

"That's good news for me." Dad turns back to Logan. "All of us men are golfing after breakfast while the girls get their nails done or shop. I look forward to getting to know you more before you marry my daughter."

I can see the horror flash on Logan's face for only a second. Logan doesn't golf. And he doesn't hang out with pretentious, misogynist men who still brag about which Ivy League school they went to all these years later.

"Actually, Dad," I start. "I was hoping to steal my fiancé so we could do a bit of exploring today."

Dad looks from Logan to me. "All right. As long as you're back in time for the rehearsal."

"We will be."

Diana calls Dad over, and I sink back into my seat. "I'll do my best to keep him from badgering you the rest of the weekend," I tell Logan.

"It's fine. I mean, he thinks we're getting married. It would be weird if he didn't try to badger me."

"That is true. We haven't spoken much, but I know my dad does care and wants me to succeed. In life. His definition of success is different from mine, and that's caused a lot of friction over the years."

"What's his definition of success?"

"Ivy League, grad school, and marrying someone who's family has clout. A trust fund is an added bonus."

Logan takes a drink and makes a face of disgust. "This is awful."

"I'll take it. The straight vodka burns."

"Be my guest." He hands me his mimosa and I take a sip.

"What is your definition of success?"

"Asking the tough questions today?" I raise my eyebrows and

then let out a breath before taking a big drink. "I just want to be happy, and I don't need some fancy job, a master's degree or a Ph.D. to do that. And I'm not going to date—let alone marry—someone that looks good on paper but doesn't make me happy either." I look down the table at Diana and Peter.

His father is an oral surgeon. His older brother is a corporate lawyer. Peter works in advertising and works with high-paying clients. I would never say my sister is stupid. Makes stupid choices sometimes, yes...but don't we all? She didn't have the grades to get into Yale, even with my father's connections. Marrying into a prestigious family is, in her eyes, one of her biggest accomplishments.

But she's happy.

"Luckily all the attention is on Diana this weekend, and she will do everything she can to keep it that way. We have free time today and then it's the rehearsal tonight and the wedding in the morning."

"Right. We do have free time today." His eyes meet mine. "How should we pass it?"

Heat rushes through me, and my throat is suddenly thick. Did he mean that to sound sexual or is my mind still stuck in the gutter? Because I'd really like to—stop.

I can't. I shouldn't.

But why the hell not?

He's my best friend.

The only steady thing I have in this crazy world, and I can't risk that.

I just can't.

CHAPTER 14

LOGAN

Danielle's eyes close in a long blink, and she reaches for her drink again. It's her go-to method when she's stressed.

"We…we could…uh…sit at, the uh, beach."

"Sure, if that's what you want to do."

"It would be relaxing." Danielle's gaze goes to her parents. Being around her family is bringing up all her insecurities. It's hard sitting here and doing nothing when I see the vulnerability reflected in her eyes. *Don't go falling in love with me, Dawson.* Her own words echo in my head.

I can't pull her close and hold her tight. I can't put my lips to hers, drinking her all in and telling her how she shouldn't worry about comparing or measuring up because she's one of the single most amazing women I've ever met.

"What about that Bamboo Forest you were talking about?" I ask.

Her lips start to curve in a smile. "You'd like to go?"

"Hell yes, I'd like to go. I looked up pictures online about it, and it looks pretty fucking cool."

"Yeah, it does. And it's only about an hour-and-fifteen-minute drive from here."

"Doesn't that mean we need to rent a car?"

She brings her drink to her lips and takes a small sip. "My dad rented a car. He won't be using it today since he's golfing. I can either ask or just go and take it. He won't even notice it's gone."

"Look at you almost committing grand theft. Maybe you are going to start a life of crime."

"Told you."

"We should have gone to Mexico instead."

She laughs. "That's too obvious."

"Ah, so it was all part of your plan?"

"Of course. I thought this all out, and you're either with me or against me."

"Oh damn." I lean back, shaking my head. "I'm with you. All the way. If not, you'll have to kill me, right?"

"Right. And then I'd throw you in the ocean and let the sharks take care of your body."

"You're ruthless, Danielle."

She narrows her eyes and nods her head. "Damn straight." She smiles and the wind blows her hair around her face. We're on an outdoor terrace, shaded from the sun. The crashing waves of the ocean echo behind us, along with happy chatter and laughter from other vacationers.

"You're spacing out," Danielle says, nudging her foot against mine under the table. I blink and tear my eyes away from the ocean, only to look at something even more beautiful.

Danielle.

"What are you thinking about?" she asks.

"How I might leave the bar in Owen's hands and never go home. It would be nice to have this year-round."

"Midwest winters can be brutal. But wouldn't you miss the change in seasons?"

I sweep my hand out at the ocean so blue it blends right in with the sky. "Not if I had this."

"Christmas and the cold just go hand in hand to me. It would be weird not to have snow around the holidays."

"We didn't have any snow last Christmas. It was forty-five degrees."

"True," she laughs. Our food comes, and we both dig in. It's the first real meal I've had since the pizza at the airport, and I'm starving. I finish everything in record time.

"It's a shame you're not joining us for golf," Peter says, coming around the table.

"I'm not much of a golfer." I set my fork and knife on my plate. "And I want to spend time with my *fiancée*." I take Danielle's hand again, smiling when I look into her eyes.

"You're a good man to follow her around shopping and getting her nails done today."

"I'm not shopping," Danielle tells him. "We're going to walk through the Bamboo Forest."

"Oh, that place looks so cool!" the bridesmaid sitting next to Danielle twists in her seat. "I watched a bunch of YouTube videos about it, and I'd love to hike it."

"Come with," Danielle offers. I don't think she really meant it and was more asking to be polite while expecting her offer to be turned down. Anyone is welcome to join us, but I didn't realize how much I was looking forward to being with just Danielle until now.

"I wish," the bridesmaid tells Danielle. "We've had these appointments for over a month, and it's what Diana wants to do."

"I heard my name." Diana's eyes widen as she looks down the table. "Talking about me?"

"Always," Danielle replies. "All gossip, of course."

Her sister laughs, smiling as she looks at Danielle. I can feel the strain between them, the slight competition I'm willing to bet was put there by their own parents without really meaning to. I understand why Danielle left, and it's almost creepy how everyone is acting like things are perfectly fine between them all.

Peter hit on Danielle at their place of work. When Danielle threatened to call him out, he proposed to Diana. And then when the truth came out, everyone sided with Peter, acting like he can't be held responsible for his actions because he's a man and Danielle should have known better than to wear something so tight and revealing to work. It hurt Danielle so much that she left without saying goodbye.

And now the whole gang is sitting here, drinking mimosas on the beach, acting like none of that ever happened. I guess when appearance is everything, you're willing to overlook a few glaringly obvious fucked-up things.

It's even weirder to think that Carol grew up in Eastwood, graduating a few years after my own parents did. Danielle doesn't talk about the fallout her mother and grandpa had, but I know things got messy after Danielle's grandmother died of cancer when her mother was a sophomore in high school. Her grandpa had a hard time dealing and drank a lot. Carol went to stay at her aunt's house in New Jersey, and things were never the same from there.

"We were talking about the Bamboo Forest trails. You know, the one with the waterfalls," the bridesmaid explains. "And how we have our nail appointments to go to instead."

"Right," Diana says with a nod. "But the trails are all muddy. So not my thing."

"And your thing is everyone's thing," Danielle says under her breath. The bridesmaid hears her and tries not to smile. "So, Diana says you just got engaged."

"Yeah." Danielle's eyes flick to mine. "Just a few weeks ago."

"Congrats! That ring is gorgeous!"

"Thanks. He did a good job." She wiggles her fingers. "I'm lucky."

The bridesmaid looks at me. "Yeah, you are."

"I'm the lucky one." I reach across the table and take Danielle's hand. It feels like the natural thing to do...but then again, so does kissing her. I force a smile and shove everything I'm feeling to the sideline where they've always been.

And I think they always will be.

"I WAS A LITTLE WORRIED DIANA WOULD PICK HIDEOUS DRESSES." Danielle does a twirl in front of the mirror. "But these are really pretty. I'd totally wear this for real." She's wearing her bridesmaid dress, and it looks beautiful on her. Though I'm pretty sure she could wrap herself up in a shower curtain and still look amazing.

The dress is a sea-green color, matching her eyes, and is shorter in the front than in the back. It's flowy and swirls around her legs as she spins.

"Looks comfortable too."

"It is, and it won't be too hot for tomorrow, which is nice." She looks down at the dress once more. "I should change, though. We need to head out if we want to make it to the Bamboo Forest. And I got the keys from my dad."

"You took them, or he gave them to you?"

"Took them."

"What a rebel," I tease.

"This is just the start. I'm thinking about swiping that really soft robe from the hotel closet too."

"I think they just charge it to your room."

"Oh." She wrinkles her nose. "Well, I'll enjoy the freebie robe for like a few hours then until they realize it's missing." Opening the dresser drawer, she grabs her clothes and goes into the bathroom to change. My stuff is still in my suitcase where I'll keep it the rest of the trip.

"Shit," I hear Danielle swear from the bathroom.

"Everything okay in there?" I call.

"My hair is stuck in the zipper."

"Need help?"

"Yes, please." She comes out of the bathroom, holding the dress up over her breasts with one hand and turns around. The zipper made it about halfway down before she ran over her hair. "I tried zipping it back up, you know, like undoing what I did. And now it's worse."

I gather her hair up in my hand, separating it from the little section that's caught in the zipper. I go to move it over her shoulder, and my fingers sweep across the soft skin on the nape of her neck. Swallowing hard, I look at the tangle of hair, trying to figure out the best way to get it out of the zipper without breaking off the long locks.

But now I'm looking at a little freckle she has on the back of her shoulder. She has tan lines that run down her back, disappearing beneath the light blue fabric of the dress.

"How bad is it?" She turns her head back, looking over her shoulder. She arches her back a bit, trying to get a better look, and her ass brushes against me, causing my cock to stir. I grit my teeth and look back at the zipper.

"Not that bad."

"Good. Because that's too much hair to cut. Also, I'm fairly certain if I broke the zipper on the dress, I'd be the dead body in the ocean. Diana won't get her hands muddy, but she has no problem getting them bloody."

"She's very, uh, focused on the wedding," I mumble. Heat radiates off of her, and being so close yet so far is the most infuriating thing in this whole fucking world. Shifting my gaze from her ass to her hair, I carefully move the zipper down, freeing a few strands of hair. A few pieces snap off, but the zipper keeps coming down, moving past the spot where it was stuck.

I should stop.

Let her finish unzipping the dress.

But I've lost control over my hands, and the zipper keeps moving down farther and farther until my fingers are hovering above the little dimple she has on her lower back. She reaches up, holding the dress with one hand, and feels her hair.

"How's the zipper? I'm almost scared to look."

"I think it's okay."

"Can you test it?" She looks over her shoulder again. "I'll make sure to keep my hair out of the way this time." Gathering her hair in one hand, she twists it and holds it out of the way. I pull the dress together, fumbling with the tiny zipper between my large fingers.

My mouth goes dry, and never in my life would I have thought zipping *up* a dress would be as much of a turn-on as *un*zipping one.

"Oh, thank God," Danielle says with a sigh once the zipper goes up to the top. She takes a step away and looks in the mirror hanging on the wall outside the bathroom. "I'll live to see another day." She comes back over and turns around. "Do you mind? I don't want to have another issue with my hair."

"Not at all."

She pulls her hair out of the way again and turns around. I stare at the little zipper, hesitating before reaching out and picking up the metal tab. I blink and see myself unzipping the dress and then spinning Danielle around. She's holding it up with hands, but when I grab her and kiss her, she lets it fall.

"Thank you, Logan," she says, stepping away. "You're a good friend."

I flash a grin. "I know. I'm the best."

She laughs and goes back into the bathroom. Once the door is closed, I sink onto the bed, mentally yelling at myself. I *am* a good fucking friend.

But I'd make an even better lover. And I'm going to prove that to her today.

CHAPTER 15

DANIELLE

I toss my bag in the back and get in the passenger seat, handing the keys to Logan. I left most of that vodka untouched on the breakfast table, but I'm still feeling a little tipsy, so having Logan drive is the safer option. Plus, I read that some of the roads are really narrow and twisty. That kind of driving would stress me out too much.

"I brought water and snacks." I pull the seatbelt over my lap and click it into place.

"Good. I'll be able to last a few hours."

I laugh. "I could never be on one of those survival shows. Going more than like six hours without eating is torture. While I'm awake, I mean. I can make an exception when I'm sleeping those solid twelve hours."

"You do not sleep for twelve hours." He backs out of the parking space. "You stay up until two or three watching YouTube videos almost every night."

"That's not true."

Logan steals a look at me, raising his eyebrows.

"Sometimes it's TV or just mindlessly scrolling through the

social media sites I don't post on that often yet still suck the happiness right out of me like a Dementor."

"Maybe not looking at those sites would be a good idea."

"Gee, you think so?" I tip my head toward his, smiling. "Though, really, I consider unplugging or even getting rid of some of my social media accounts altogether." I watch the resort get smaller and smaller in the rear-view mirror. I haven't checked any of my social media since we landed, and I'm quite proud of myself for that. Waking up, grabbing my phone, and starting my day by comparing myself to others is really self-defeating and not worth it at all.

It's easy to fake a perfect life in fifteen-second clips or with a posed—and photoshopped—image. Hell, even I can make my life look fulfilling and amazing and not full of fuck-up moments.

"You should," Logan says. "If I didn't run Getaway's social media, I wouldn't be online much at all. Well, other than to read articles and find spoiler-filled memes to send to Dean. He's always behind in whatever show we're watching."

"Poor Dean."

"He brings it upon himself." Logan's eyes light up. "And if he'd read the fucking books said shows were based on, I couldn't spoil it at all."

"Yeah, but who has time to read?" I huff, dramatically rolling my eyes.

Logan just shakes his head. He reads several books a week, and I've found him in the office with a book, hiding away from the busy crowd at the bar more than once. I turn on the radio, flipping through stations until I find one we both like. Then I turn up the radio and watch the gorgeous island pass by.

The breeze picks up a bit when we get to the other side of the island, and gray clouds overhead bring the promise of rain. We park along the side of the road and get out. There are a few other cars parked along the road as well, but right now, everything is silent.

"So, from what I read online," I start, looking around, "we need to find an access point, which is not really anything bigger than a deer trail."

Logan locks the car and looks at the foliage lining the road. "There's one." He points to a trail that's so narrow it's easy to miss. I start forward but hesitate, getting a flash of running into thick spider webs as I ran through rows of corn back when I was a kid.

"Want me to go first and break the spider webs?"

"How did you know that's what I was thinking?"

Logan's eyes meet mine, and my heart gets all fluttery again. "You've brought up that emotionally scarring story of running into what you called a banana spider even though they live in the tropics in South America."

"It was big and very yellow."

Logan chuckles and steps off the road, leading the way to the little path. We only make it a few feet before feeling like we've been transported away from a busy tourist site to the middle of a jungle, surrounded by nothing but wildlife and trees. We continue on the path, which is muddy like Diana feared, for a bit and then emerge onto the bigger path. A group of people are a few yards ahead of us, talking and taking selfies every few feet.

"Hang on a second." I grab Logan's wrist, pulling him back toward me. It was meant to be an innocent gesture, but wrapping my fingers around his arm stirs something inside of me. I've touched Logan before—all friendly touches, of course—and I've never gotten this kind of response before.

Because right now, feeling his warm skin under my fingers is causing my sensitive parts to swell with desire. It's hot and humid under the thick of branches and leaves, but a chill makes its way through me.

"What?" Logan twists his hand, breaking out of my hold. But he doesn't move away like he normally would. No, this time he flips his hand over and curls his fingers over mine. I'm well aware we're standing here, literally doing nothing more than hold hands.

And yet, he was able to get such a strong physical reaction out of me.

"I, uh…uh…" What was I doing? Why did I reach for Logan again? Oh right. "Those people up there."

"What about them?"

"I like feeling like we're actually out exploring the jungle and wanted to put some distance between us and them."

"Okay." He watches the little group slowly move down the trail. "We shouldn't wait too long, though, or someone will be behind us. Though if you really wanted to feel like you're exploring the jungle, we should go off the path."

"They have the path here for a reason. We might get in trouble if we move off the trail."

"Maybe you should rethink your life of crime. If veering off a path in a park is pushing it for you, then how are you going to handle all the smuggling and murder?"

I come to a dead stop, crossing my arms over my chest, waiting for Logan to turn around before I make my next overly dramatic move.

"We should—" he starts but cuts off when he realizes I've stopped walking behind him. Narrowing my eyes, I take a big step off the path. Amused, Logan watches as I take another step off the path. And another.

And another.

"I'm a rebel." I whirl around and march forward, but this time I really do walk right into a spider web. I bring my hands up, frantically trying to get the web off me and spin around. I didn't see Logan rush over to help me, and I end up whacking him hard in the face.

"Shit, I'm so sorry!" I jerk back, slip on wet leaves, and my feet go right out from under me. I land in thick mud, and Logan can't stop laughing. "Jerk!"

"Here." He extends his hand, still laughing, and helps me to my feet. I turn around, looking at my butt. "It looks like you shit your pants."

I purse my lips and try to glare but then start laughing too. "And to think I felt bad for hitting you."

"You barely grazed me. Also, there's a spider in your hair."

Suddenly looking like there's poop on my pants is the least of my worries. Instead of freaking out, I freeze. Logan reaches forward, pulling a spider out of my hair by one leg. He holds it up so I can see and then tosses it aside.

I shudder. "I need to shower for like a week now. In hot water. And bleach."

"Get used to the bugs, princess. You never know when you're going to have to go on the lam once you start your crime ring."

"Princess?" I put my hand on my hip and glare at Logan. His brown eyes are shining, and that smile on his face is doing bad things to me right now. Bending down, I scoop up a handful of mud and raise my arm back.

"You wouldn't dare."

"Oh, I would. I mean, I will." I throw the mud at Logan, who easily dodges out of the way. He slips, but recovers, and jumps across a tangle of greenery. Both of my hands are muddy from falling. I can still get him.

I take off after him, laughing as I reach out with muddy fingers. Logan dodges between bamboo shoots, moving through the thick forest with ease. Damn him and his natural athletic ability. My hair catches on a piece of bamboo, and I slow, turning to see how bad it's tangled before pulling it free. When I start forward again, I don't see Logan.

Coming to a dead stop, I look around and realize I have no idea which direction the path is in. We could have only come in a few yards away from the trail, but the forest is so thick it's hard to see through.

Holding my breath, I slowly turn around, listening for any

sounds of life. And then something comes crashing through the trees behind me. Logan jumps out at me, and I let out a little shriek as I lunge forward, ready to smear mud on his face. He catches my wrist, blocking my attempt to run my fingers down his cheek.

"Nice try!"

"I know, right?" I bring my other hand up and pat his cheek.

"Dammit," he laughs.

"Now we're even."

"Even? You're the klutz who fell in the mud." He lets go or my wrist and brings his hand up, pushing a loose strand of hair back out of my face. I drop my hand from his face and rest it on his shoulder. Logan steps in a little closer and the heat coming off of him is a hundred times more intense than the heat of this whole damn island.

He takes in a breath. It's a simple gesture—a necessary one—yet with my hand on his shoulder, I feel every muscle moving under my fingers. I swallow hard, not sure if I'm going to be able to resist him for much longer.

I want him to kiss me as much as I don't.

The breeze picks up, rattling through the bamboo around us. Logan rests his other hand on my waist. Looking into his eyes, I slowly run my hand down, splaying my fingers over his peck.

Damn him and his muscles.

And the way the faint scent of his cologne is mixing with the fresh scent of the forest.

"Are we lost?" I ask, voice coming out a faint whisper.

Logan widens his stance and presses his fingers into my skin. "Depends."

"On what?"

"On what you consider lost."

My lips curve into a smile. "Not knowing where we are."

"Then yes, we're lost."

"Should I be worried?"

"Nah, I think we're—oh, shit another spider!"

I jump forward, crashing into him. "That's not funny!" He's laughing, and brings his arms in, folding them around me. Warmth rushes through me, tingling my core and making me never want to move away from him.

"You do know spiders crawl all over you at night, right?"

I tip my head up. "I refuse to believe that." My arms are smashed between my chest and Logan's, and my muscles are twitching as I resist wrapping them around his torso. It's been a while since I've snuggled or cuddled with anyone, and being close to Logan feels amazing right now.

But it's more than that, and I know it.

"You eat them in your sleep too."

"I have never in my life eaten a spider."

"Keep telling yourself that."

"I will. And I will believe it until the day I die."

Logan chuckles, and the laughter rumbles his chest, which I'm still very much up against. My heart threatens to take over, but that traitor has led me down the path of disappointment and pain way too many times before.

That's why I left.

And why I left is why I met Logan.

Maybe things do happen for a reason.

But I swore I'd listen to my head instead of my heart, though right now…right now my head can't come up with a single reason not to give in. Not to tip my head up and lock eyes with Logan. To finally feel what those full lips would feel like against mine.

My heart hammers away in my chest, so fast I'm sure Logan can feel it. I can feel his gaze on me, and I know if I look up this will be it.

The moment our friendship changes forever.

CHAPTER 16

DANIELLE

It terrifies me as much as it excites me, and my entire body yearns to feel his right up against mine. I blink, swallow hard, and look up. Logan's eyes meet mine, and the way he's looking at me makes me want to melt into a puddle on the forest floor. If he wasn't holding onto me, there's a good chance my knees would have given out.

All my life, I've wanted someone to look at me the way Logan is looking at me right now. Like he can't wait to strip me down and run his hands all over my body. Like he's going to take all night pleasing me. Like I'm the only woman he ever wants to look at ever again.

Looking at me like I matter.

The wind blows through again, followed by fat raindrops. Logan hugs me tighter, shielding me from the rain with his own body.

"What the hell? It was sunny when we left." This time I do slip my arms around him.

"We're on the other side of the island now."

"Crazy how just an hour or so drive can make that much of a difference."

The wind gusts again, but no more rain falls down. Logan loosens his grip. "Gotta love those little cloud bursts." He lets his arms fall to the side.

"Hey, I'll take it." I step back and smooth out my shirt, trying and failing to suck in air. What the hell just happened? And I don't mean with the weather. Logan and I were so close—literally—and everything felt so right.

But just like the rain, the moment came and passed.

"For real," I start, hardly able to look at Logan without blood rushing through me. "Are we lost?"

"I'm sure we can find the path again."

"So we're lost."

"I'll admit we're lost when you admit you eat spiders in your sleep."

"Fine. We're not lost. We're just…not where we thought we'd be."

"That's an interesting way to look at things."

"It is," I agree as the words actually hit me. I've felt lost for so long because I wasn't where I thought I'd be in life. I'm edging thirty, with a business degree from Yale, a few years of grad school under my belt, and yet I'm waiting tables and tending the bar in a small town and living with my grandpa.

But I like Eastwood, and I like working at Getaway. I enjoy eating dinner with Grandpa. It makes my heart full knowing he's happy to have family back in the house. I'm so grateful I met Logan and Owen and the rest of their crazy family. I reconnected with Rebecca and her children.

It seems crazy to say I'm happy and didn't realize it, but that's exactly what I am. I've been so consumed with "getting back on track" and making my next big move, I lost sight of what was going on around me.

And I thought I didn't have tunnel vision.

Logan leads the way, breaking any spiderwebs that I might walk through, and we hike through the forest in silence for a few minutes. It's anything but awkward, though. I haven't felt this kind of mental peace in years.

"Do you hear that?" Logan asks, turning around. We both come to a stop.

"Voices."

Logan holds out his hand for me to take. I don't hesitate. I reach forward and slip my fingers through his. We trek a few yards through the thick bamboo trees and emerge onto the path, startling the tourists walking ahead of us.

We're back on the main path, and I don't let go of Logan's hand.

~

I STAND AT THE EDGE OF A ROCKY STREAM, STARING UP AT A waterfall. Logan is at my side, and we finally caved and took a few selfies. I even uploaded one to my Instagram stories. The group of hikers who were ahead of us have already crossed the stream, and for the time being, Logan and I are alone in front of the first waterfall.

"It's so beautiful."

"Yeah," Logan agrees. "It is. And it's louder than I expected."

Smiling, I look away from the fall to look at his handsome face. "It is quite intense. Ready to cross now?"

He holds out his hand for me to take again. "Hell yeah."

We carefully make our way over the slippery rocks, and I somehow manage to not fall in. Though I'm already covered in mud. What's a little water going to hurt?

We continue along the path until we reach the second falls. This time, we're not alone, and the group that was ahead of us is perching on rocks and wading into the cool water for pictures. I snap a few pictures, and make Logan pose for just one selfie with me. He puts his arm around me, and we both smile at the camera.

You wouldn't know we weren't a real couple by the looks of it.

And by the feel of it...I don't want to think about it and complicate things.

"We have to climb up that." Logan points to a rather steep and slick hillside. The trail is small and narrow and easy to miss.

"Looks easy," I say apprehensively, but there's no way I'm giving up. I might not be the most athletic person or have the best balance or coordination, but I'm certain I can get myself up that path.

"Go first," Logan tells me. "If you slip, I'll catch you."

"You just want to check out my butt."

"I've been checking out your butt this whole time."

"You've been in front of me," I retort.

"That just goes to show how good I am."

Shaking my head, I grab onto a stalk of bamboo and use it to steady myself as I start up the rocky hill. There are little divots in the stone, and I try to keep my feet in them as I move up. My feet slip a few times, and I'm even more glad I wore sensible shoes over sandals. I recover, moving slower yet feeling reassured that Logan is behind me.

We come down through the forest and emerge into a small clearing of grey rocks that surround another waterfall.

"Wow," Logan says, letting out a breath. Wow is right. Water cascades down a jumble of rocks, pouring into a large pool. Greenery hugs the dark rocks that surround the water.

We've been hiking for what feels like hours. I'm hot, sweaty, and desperately thirsty. Drinking this morning and then going on a difficult hike was not a good idea. Logan takes the backpack off, and we find a flat rock to sit on.

"How you doing?" he asks, handing me a water bottle.

"Do I look rough or something?"

He laughs. "Do you really want me to answer that?"

"Shut up, jerk." I twist the cap off the water and drink half the bottle. "That feels better. And now I'm ready for a nap." Logan is sitting close next to me, and putting my head on his shoulder sounds like a good idea. Though I would probably fall asleep for sure that way.

"There's a good chance my dad is going to try and steal you away after the rehearsal tonight," I warn Logan.

"Why would he—oh, right. I almost forgot we're pretending. It doesn't feel like we are." He sets his water bottle down and gets up, pulling his shirt over his head before I have a chance to even process what he just said. The muscles in his back flex and he brings his arm down, dropping it down. "You coming?" he asks as he heads toward the water. I take another big drink and put the cap back on, standing and shimmying out of my shorts. I pull my shirt over my head, tossing it on the rock with our other clothes.

Logan's already waist-deep by the time I get to the water. It's cool but feels amazing since I'm so sweaty.

"This really is paradise." Logan swims forward before plunging under the water.

"It is." I'm slow going down into the water, knowing getting my breasts in the cold water is going to be the worst part. I should just grit my teeth and dive in too. I ease in and then chicken out, standing back up.

And then Logan grabs my arm, pulling me toward him and into the water. He laughs as he floats onto his back, bringing me with him. The cold water shocks me, and I hook my arms around his shoulders. He stands up, spinning me around, and then plunges back into the water.

"Feels good, doesn't it?"

My heart is in my throat. "Yeah, it does."

The water feels good.

Logan feels even better, and now I'm feeling confused because my heart and my head are crossing paths. I've been pretending Logan is my fiancé. Acting like we're a happy, loving couple.

But other than talking about a wedding that's not going to happen, things really don't seem that different between us.

Except this…having Logan's arms around me. I'm wearing a

bright yellow bikini and he has on swim trunks. My skin is against his, and I'm all too aware of the thin layer of material that separates his cock from me.

"I could stay here all day." Keeping one arm around Logan's neck, I extend the other out and run my fingers along the surface of the water.

"Me too. But I want more food."

"There's supposed to be a farm truck not far from where we parked. Or at least that's what I read online."

"That sounds familiar. I might have watched a few YouTube videos about the whole Road to Hana drive."

I bring my other arm back in and rest my hand on Logan's shoulder. My heart hasn't stopped hammering since he pulled me into the water.

"You're so thorough."

"I like to have all my bases covered."

Dammit. Why does everything sound so sexual right now? I drop my eyes to Logan's chest and fight the temptation to bring my body closer and get a feel of his cock through his swim trunks. I've seen him in sweatpants, athletic shorts, and pajama pants. And while I told myself I shouldn't steal glances, I have.

I so have, and I'll just say I won't be disappointed.

"Want to do that rope swing?" Logan asks as he moves his hand from my waist to the small of my back. I'm hot all over again despite the cold water. Does he even know what he's doing to me? He has to...right?

We're not walking the line of really good friends anymore. His hands are on me. My hands are on him. My mind is on his cock, and I want that cock—*fuck*. I need to fucking stop.

"I'm the type of person who would slip and fall. But yeah, let's do it!"

Logan laughs and makes no attempt to let me go. "Just hold on and let go when I tell you to. You'll be fine."

"I don't have much upper body strength," I say seriously. "Are you sure I'll be able to hold on long enough to swing out past the point of falling to my death?"

"That kid just went for the third time. You'll survive."

"My life is in your hands, Dawson."

He brings his hands back to my waist, gripping it tight. "I think I can handle that."

If there ever was a time for an epic first kiss, this would be it. Like in any good romance movie, the cameras would pan in slowly, capturing the beauty of the landscape while showcasing the passion and desire in the lovers' eyes. Lips would part, one last breath would be exchanged before eyes shut.

My tongue darts out, wetting my lips. Heat radiates through me, and my core is so hot, so desperate to feel more, it's a wonder Logan can't feel it. I've never felt more grounded than I do right now, floating in cool water in front of a waterfall and in Logan's arms.

My whole life was laid out before me. I was told what to do every step of the way. I never had a chance to break out on my own, and when I did, I messed up. I thought I was lost. I thought I was making mistakes.

I didn't realize that the map was in my hands the whole time, and I was the one holding the pen, ready to draw a new road. I thought I was lost, but for the last year, I've been exactly where I need to be.

Right here, right in front of Logan Dawson.

CHAPTER 17

LOGAN

I pride myself on being a rational person. Thinking things through and not taking risks has got me this far in life relatively unscathed. And right now?

Right now I want to kiss Danielle.

I want to hold her close and never let go.

But that's a risk, isn't it?

She's my best friend, has made it clear she's not interested in dating anyone, and doesn't even want to stay in Eastwood. Eastwood is my home. All my family is there…yet I'd follow Danielle anywhere.

I lower my gaze from her eyes to her lips, well aware that this might be the single most stupid decision I've ever made. But sometimes you have to take risks to reap the reward.

But a million *what-ifs* go through my mind, and for each one, I can find a logical reason to call bullshit.

What if things are awkward between us? *It's not like they haven't been before. We'll get over it.*

What if the kiss is bad? *There's no chance in Hell it's going to be bad.*

What if she doesn't want me to kiss her? *All the signs are here: she wants this as much as I do.*

That's it. I'm doing it. It's now or never. Danielle's eyes start to close. I inhale and bring my face to hers.

"Excuse me?"

I come to a stop, lips just inches away from Danielle's.

"Could you take our picture?"

What. The. Fuck.

I open my eyes and turn my head, seeing a young couple holding out a phone.

"We're celebrating our engagement too," the girl says, looking away from me and into her girlfriend's eyes. Too? Oh right. Danielle has that big-ass fake diamond on her finger. I open my mouth, but no sound comes out. Everything inside of me is still in motion, set on finally kissing Danielle.

"Yeah," Danielle says. "Congrats on your engagement." Her voice is breathy, like she's feeling the same way I am.

"Thank you," the girl with short blonde hair squeals. "And you too. I think. You have that look in your eyes, and that ring is stunning!"

Danielle looks back at me, and the lie sits heavy in my stomach. It's not fun pretending anymore.

"I'm a lucky guy," I say, forcing myself to play the part I committed to. The lie is hanging on by a thread, and I'm not sure I can do this anymore. Because nothing I'm saying feels like a lie.

I am in love with Danielle. Having her this close yet so far hurts more than I ever thought it could.

"I'm the lucky one," Danielle goes on, flashing a smile. How is this easy for her? Maybe she doesn't feel the same like I hoped. She takes the phone and snaps a few photos for the newly engaged couple. They take their phone back and walk out of the water.

"So, the rope swing," I start, looking from Danielle to the rope. "You want to try it?"

"I still think I'm going to get hurt."

"I'll help you."

She wraps her arms around my neck again, pulling herself close. Her breasts press up against my chest, and I can feel her pert nipples through the thin padding on her swimsuit.

This woman is going to kill me.

"I'm a little scared of heights."

"It's not that high," I counter. "I'll go first. Prove to you that if I can do it—and that six-year-old over there—then you can do it."

"That kid is at least twelve." She releases me and falls back into the water, floating on her back. "And yes, let's try this. But if I die, I'm haunting you for the rest of your life."

"I don't believe in ghosts."

"Oh, you will once my angry spirit starts breaking all the top-shelf bottles of booze at the bar. But I'll start out way more subtle than that. Dex will wake up at night, staring at the wall growling. You'll start to wonder, getting just a little freaked out. Then things will go missing. Doors will shut on their own, along with flickering lights."

"You've really thought this out."

"I've wished angry spirits on people before. It's fun imagining what would happen."

I laugh. "You know you sound a little crazy every now and then."

"You say that like it's a bad thing?"

I shake my head and swim forward. "It's not at all. It's one of the many things I like about you."

"Many?" She follows me out of the water, wringing out her hair.

"What? That's a surprise?"

She shrugs, and I hate how downtrodden she gets every now and then, like she can't see her own worth. It doesn't happen very often, and I know she works hard to keep her chin up no matter what is going on.

I help Danielle up the slick path to the rope swing. One person is ahead of us, and we watch them grab on, take a running leap, and then plunge into the water.

"Are you sure it's deep enough?" Danielle asks, creeping toward the edge of the overhang. The rope swings back and I grab it.

"I'll find out."

Danielle lets out a gasp as I run and jump, swinging out over the water before letting go. I sink below the surface and pop right back up, treading water as I look at Danielle.

"Your turn," I call.

She crosses her arms over her body and shakes her head.

"Don't make me use the line."

"What line?" She looks down into the water at me.

I hold one hand up toward her. "Do you trust me?" *Aladdin* is her favorite movie, and that line gets her every time.

Pursing her lips, her eyes lock with me. Then her whole body relaxes. "Yes, I trust you." She grabs the rope and takes a few paces back, moving out of my line of sight. I know she's afraid of falling, but she has nothing to fear. I'm right here to catch her.

I'll always be here.

I move out of the way and watch her run to the edge of the rock. It's only when she jumps that I notice she wrapped her arm awkwardly around the rope, probably done to ensure she'll be able to hang on.

"Let go!" I yell, wincing since I know that rope is going to burn as she falls. She squeezes her eyes shut and free falls into the water. I swim back over right as she pops up from the water.

"That was so fun!" she says with a big smile on her face. "I don't know why I was so scared!"

"How's your arm?" We swim back to shallower water.

"My arm?"

"You don't have a rope burn?"

She brings her left arm up. Her forearm is raw and little beads of blood pool on her skin. "Oh shit. I didn't even feel that."

I take her arm in my hands, bringing it closer. "It's just a surface scrape. You'll be fine, but that kind of thing can hurt."

"I have a battle wound." She tosses her head up, trying to look tough. We both laugh. "As long as it doesn't get infected from being in this water, I'm good."

"Let's pretend this water is clean and filtered. It's coming from a waterfall. People pay top dollar to drink pure water like this."

Danielle laughs, looking down at her arm once more before sticking it back under the water. "I can live with that."

"You did awesome," I tell her, knowing she was scared to jump.

"Thanks. I hesitated. I want to go again and not hesitate this time."

"Don't wrap your arm around the rope this time."

"Come with me?"

"Of course."

We go back up the slippery rocks to the rope. Danielle goes first this time, and she doesn't hesitate, not at all. I jump in after her, and we spend a while just floating and swimming around in the water before getting out and swinging off the rope again.

Back on the rocks, we eat the rest of the snacks Danielle packed for us, drying off in the sun that's streaming down on us now. She finishes her water and stretches her arms over her head, looking up at the bright sky.

"Want to try and find that food stand next?" she asks.

"You're really asking if I want to try and find food?"

She laughs. "Good point. When aren't you hungry?" Her eyes glimmer when they meet mine. "No wonder your mom is such a good cook. She had four of you boys growing up."

"And Quinn. She can eat like the rest of us."

"Having one older sister growing up was rough enough. I can't imagine having four older brothers."

"It made her tough," I laugh.

"That's for sure." Danielle unbraids her hair and piles it all up on the top of her head in a messy bun.

"Isn't that heavy?" I ask, motioning to her hair. "Especially when it's wet?"

"Yeah, but I guess I'm used to it. I've always had long hair. I'd miss it way too much to cut even though I'm so tempted every now and then."

"It would drive me crazy."

"Eh, it's not too bad. I won't miss finding hairs in my butt crack though."

"What?"

Danielle laughs and grabs her shorts from the rock. "It happens to everyone with long hair, trust me. Hair just like falls out and goes right down in between my butt cheeks."

"You're being serious?"

"Yes! Ask anyone with long hair."

I shake my head. "I am not asking anyone if they pull hair out of their ass."

"Not really out of your ass, just the crack." She pulls her shirt over her head and takes another lingering look at the waterfall. "I'm starving."

"I didn't know talking about pulling hair out of your crack could be so appetizing."

A smile pulls up her face. My God…this woman is so beautiful. "You're not the only one who is always hungry, Dawson."

"Then let's go get something to eat." I look at my watch. "We need to hurry, though."

"I don't even know what time it is. It feels like we just got here while at the same time I know we've spent a decent amount of time here already. Do we have time to get food?"

"If we hurry, we should be fine."

"Should be?"

I stand, reaching for my shirt. "Let's not get lost this time."

"You admitted we were lost." She puts her shorts back on.

"Call it what you will," I chuckle. "But we got here, right?"

Danielle freezes, taking her hands off the button she was about to snap into place and looks into my eyes. My heart is in my throat, and I swallow hard, pushing it back down. "You are right," she says, and she gets a distant look in her eyes. She looks out at the water again, and I watch as different emotions dance across her face. "We got here."

She's not just talking about the waterfall, and I wait for her to go on. But she doesn't, and she finishes buttoning her jean shorts and then picks up the backpack, putting it on. I hold out my arm, and she loops her arm through mine. We start toward the trail again, stopping to let a large group of hikers coming up to the water pass us by. They're seeing the waterfall for the first time, and their reactions are pretty priceless.

"Tourists," Danielle says, shaking her head. "You know I come here once and I'm basically an expert. Though I do wish I could come back and finish the rest of the Road to Hana."

"We will," I tell her, deciding it right then and there.

"When? The wedding is tomorrow and we're leaving the next day."

"I didn't mean this trip. We'll come back to Hawaii. Do things on our terms."

She comes to a halt, turning to look at me. Her sea-green eyes are wide, and her face is slack with shock.

Then she smiles.

The jingling of dog tags gets our attention, and a very muddy yellow lab comes barreling down the path, dragging his leash behind him.

"Brody!" someone yells. "Get back here!"

Danielle goes to pick up the leash and the dog whirls around, jumping on her and smearing mud all over her top.

"Hey, buddy," she says, petting the dog, whose tail is wagging hard, making his whole butt wiggle. It reminds me of Dexter, and I don't care how lame it makes me to admit I miss my dog right now.

"I'm so sorry," Brody's owner says, panting as he slows to a walk and grabs the leash. "Brody, down!"

"It's okay," Danielle says, giving Brody one more pet before he tries to come and jump on me. "I like dogs."

I scratch Brody under the chin, getting mud on my hands but not caring. Dex would have a hay-day on this trail too and would be just as muddy if not muddier.

"He's only a year old and has too much energy." The owner struggles to hold onto Brody, who gets excited to see the water.

"He's a sweet boy," Danielle tells him.

"He's lucky he is." The owner shakes his head. "Sorry you got all muddy."

Danielle waves her hand in the air. "I was already muddy before. It's no big deal."

Brody pulls his owner forward to the water, and Danielle loops her arm through mine again. "And now you're thinking about Dex, aren't you?"

"How'd you know?"

"Dex is to you what cats are to Quinn."

I raise an eyebrow. "I am not that borderline certifiable."

"Depends on who you're asking."

Shaking my head, I start forward. "We need to get going if we want to stop at the farm truck."

THE WAY BACK TO THE ROAD WASN'T MUCH EASIER THAN THE WAY up to the waterfalls. Danielle kept up, though, and pushed forward every time I suggested we slow. Her childhood wasn't spent roaming through cornfields and woods like mine was.

There's a small line at the farm truck, and Danielle is so excited to buy some sort of sugarcane drink she read about online I don't have the heart to tell her we're really cutting it close on time. Assuming we don't hit any snags on the way back to the resort, we'll have just enough time to change and run downstairs to the lobby to meet everyone for the rehearsal.

We order a ton of fruit and a few specialty items we're told you can only get at this location, and slowly walk through a mowed clearing as we eat.

"Thank you, Logan," Danielle says, thanking me for the millionth time.

"You don't have to keep thanking me, Danielle. It's not like it's torture being here with you, even though you are pretty terrible to be around every now and then."

Danielle punches me in the shoulder. "Right? I'm the worst."

We both laugh, and Danielle holds out her drink, telling me I have to try it.

"Isn't that amazing?"

"It's really sweet, but yeah, that's good. I want to add some rum to it."

"Ohhh now that would be good."

We finish our food and walk back to the car. Danielle looks through the photos she took on the hike, and then puts her phone down, resting her head against the seat. We make it another mile or so before she dozes off, which is a good thing, because we run into a bit of a traffic jam. And by traffic jam, I mean a few cows wandered off the grassy hillside and are standing in the road. It's not an uncommon thing to have happen back home, and while the people in the car ahead of us are sitting there not knowing what to do, I put our car in park and get out.

It takes a few minutes to shoo the cows away, and Danielle wakes up when I get back in.

"I didn't mean to fall asleep," she grumbles. "Were you out of the car?

"Yeah." I pull my seatbelt back on. "There were cows in the road."

"That's random, and not what I expected to hear. I almost forget people have to have normal lives in order to live here."

"Right? It's easy to think it's nothing but a tropical utopia all the time."

"Exactly." She looks at the clock. "Oh shit."

"Yeah…We'll make it. I think."

CHAPTER 18

DANIELLE

"Reassuring." I watch another minute tick by. I don't want to be that asshole who's late for her own sister's rehearsal dinner. Though I'd rather be late for this than her actual wedding.

"I'll drop you off and then just go. I'll meet you at the restaurant with your clothes. What do you want to wear?"

"I brought a light blue dress with a floral pattern on it to wear tonight."

"I'll figure it out," Logan tells me.

"I need underwear too." I make a face. "If you can handle that. The strings on my bikini bottoms will stick out funny."

Logan gives a casual shrug. "Just don't wear underwear."

"What if it's a little breezy on the shore?"

"Then we'll all get a free show."

"Hey, I don't give anything away for free."

Logan laughs, and I shift in my seat, feeling anxious to get back to the hotel. I nervously scroll through social media, trying to pass the time as we drive back around the island and to the hotel. Logan pulls into the parking lot with six minutes to spare.

"Just come with me," I tell him, unbuckling my seatbelt. "I'll change after the rehearsal."

"Are you sure?"

"Yeah. I'm here, and there are worse things than being a little messy. It's not the actual wedding."

Logan nods and parks the car. Then we get out and rush to the lobby. Everyone is there, and my phone rings right as I step in. It's my mother, no doubt wondering where I am.

"We're here!" I say, bringing my hand up in a wave. My mom whirls around, looking relieved…until she sees me.

"What the hell happened to you?" she exclaims. Her hair is all done up, and her makeup has no doubt been professionally applied.

"We went hiking." I smile. "And saw waterfalls and jumped off a cliff. Well, not really a cliff. It wasn't that steep. But it was incredible!"

"You're dirty."

I look down, having forgotten about the paw prints. "Shoot. Right. There was a dog."

"Go change."

"Don't we have to get started?" I ask, looking up. It's then I realize Diana's not here yet. "Where's Di?"

"At the salon. There was an issue with her hair, and if that's any indication of how tomorrow's going to go…Your poor sister was so upset and couldn't stop crying. She missed her nail appointment, and they're just now finishing up with her." My mother's lips form a thin line, and she shakes her head. I get it, I really do. Weddings are important. You put more time and money into one single day than you do to a bunch of days added up.

I want my own wedding to run smoothly. I want things to all go according to plan, and I want to look flawless. But I can't help but think my sister is being dramatic. That when it's all said and down, it should come down to how much she loves Peter and how they can't wait to spend the rest of their lives together.

What you look like today isn't going to matter ten years from now.

"I'll be down in like ten minutes," I tell my mom, and reach behind me for Logan's hand. We practically run down the hall and into our hotel room. Logan uses the bathroom while I grab my dress, and then we switch to get dressed. I shut the bathroom door behind me and strip down, stepping into the shower before the water fully warms up. I wash away the sweat and mud, and then get out, toweling off in record time.

I get dressed, wrap my hair in a towel, and put on one swipe of shimmery eye shadow and mascara. Then I move around like a maniac to braid my wet hair, put on deodorant, and grab my lip gloss.

"You look beautiful," Logan says when I emerge from the bathroom.

"Really?"

"Yeah," he laughs. "You don't need to do yourself all up to look good, Danielle. I think you always look good."

He's told me that before, and he's never been shy with the compliments. But there's something different about them now, something that makes my stomach flutter and my pussy contract with want. Heat floods my veins.

"You look good too."

"Oh, I know I do." He flashes a cocky grin and holds out his hand. "Ready?"

"As I'll ever be." I pick up my purse and go out the hotel room door, rushing hand in hand with Logan to the elevator. We get back into the lobby with a few minutes to spare as everyone waits for Diana. When she and Peter finally come down, everyone coos over her, telling her how pretty she is and how amazing her hair looks.

My sister is pretty, and I smile when I see her. "You look beautiful," I say, walking over.

"Thanks." Diana beams. Then she looks at my arm. "What is this?" Her eyes go wide, and at first, I think she's being a concerned older sister. "This is going to stand out in the photos!" And then I realize she's more concerned about how I'll look standing up at the altar with her.

"It's not that bad." I look down at the red marks on my arm. "I won't be so red tomorrow."

"You're going to have to cover it with makeup."

Smearing makeup all over the wound is the last thing I want to do, but I smile and nod anyway, because that's the kind of person I am. It's Diana's wedding. I should do all that I can to accommodate her…right?

Well, as long as it's within reason. I'm not cutting my hair, but I can dust some powder over the scratches as long as they've scabbed over, which they will by the morning. With a huff, Diana goes over to her friends, leaving me feeling a little sad at the relationship we don't have.

We've never really had one if I'm being honest with myself. Once Dad set his sights on getting me into Yale and following the path he laid out for me, Diana went on the defense and did everything she could to get attention, which usually got her into trouble. And then, along with being the "smart one," I was the good girl too.

Logan comes up behind me, and his hand lands on the small of my back. My stomach does a weird flip-flop thing and my pulse quickens. I turn my head to look at his handsome face. His hair is windswept and messy but looks so damn good on him. He got tanner just from that time outside, which I'm totally not jealous about at all.

My mother calls for everyone to follow her, and we start walking through the hotel. There's a wedding going on tonight on the beach where Diana and Peter's ceremony will be held tomorrow, so the rehearsal is taking place on another part of the lawn right outside the resort.

Logan takes my hand in his. "Gotta uphold appearances, right?" he asks quietly.

"Right." I give his hand a squeeze.

"Please tell me we're eating first."

"Sorry," I reply. "Rehearsal first. I'm starving too. You're not in the wedding party, so you don't have to watch us walk down a fake aisle over and over."

"So you're saying I can get something to eat."

"I am. And I'm also saying you could bring me something to snack on."

He smiles and pulls his hand from mine. "I'll be right back then."

The wedding planner gets us lined up, going over a few things before we do our trial run. We're paired up by height, and now I'm standing next to Peter's brother.

"Hi," I say. "I'm Danielle. Diana's sister."

"I thought so. You two look alike. I'm Mike."

"Nice to meet you."

"Are you enjoying the island?"

I nod, looking past him to the outdoor bar where Logan went. "I am. A lot. You?"

"I've enjoyed it more in the past," he laughs. "We brought our kids this time, and they're still a little young to go out and explore."

"How old are they?"

"Seven and five."

"Oh wow, you must have your hands full."

Mike nods. "At least the weather is nice, right? They've played on the beach all day today. I have sand in places I didn't know could get sandy."

I chuckle and wonder if Mike is a standup guy like he seems right now, or if he's a dirtbag like Peter. It's not fair to judge his whole family based on his shitty behavior. I'm nothing like the rest of my family, after all.

We practice walking down the aisle three times. My left arm sports the scratches, Diana reminds me all three times to keep my body angled so the "gross wounds" don't show on anyone's photos they might take and upload to social media before she has a chance to "request they edit them."

I spot Logan after the third run and sneak out of the line up to go over to him.

"You are the best!" I tell him, grabbing a French fry and dipping it into ranch. He knows I prefer it to ketchup.

"And I got you a strawberry margarita."

"You know me so well." I pick up the drink, suck down a mouthful, and then go back to the line. We walk down the aisle and line up again. Diana wants to run through everything once more, and I rush back over to Logan, quickly eating a few more fries before picking up the margarita.

The wedding planner says only Diana and Peter need to take a practice run again and the rest of us can relax. I sit next to Logan and pull my phone from my purse as I eat a few more fries. I texted Grandpa early today but haven't actually spoken to him.

"Hey, kiddo," he answers. "Having fun?"

"I am, actually. How are things at home?"

"I'm hardly managing without you, which is what you wanted to hear, right?"

"Maybe just a little."

"It's quiet without you here. And there's been a bottle of wine in the fridge since last night that's still full."

"Hey," I say with a laugh. "I don't like wine that much." Logan hears and rolls his eyes at me. "I'm glad you're doing all right without me. But the real question is how's the bar? Did it fall into ruins without Logan there to manage things?"

Grandpa laughs, and his laugh turns into a cough. That's been happening to him lately. "I went there last night. Busy as ever."

"That's good. I don't know the last time Owen actually worked at work."

Logan nods in agreement and picks up the margarita, taking a big drink.

"Enjoy the rest of your time in Hawaii."

"I will, Grandpa."

"And Ellie?"

"Yeah?"

"Stop worrying and follow your heart." He ends the call after that, leaving me to think about his words. Logan and I share the rest of the margarita, and when he gets up to recycle the plastic cup, the bridesmaid that was talking to me this morning comes over.

"Hey!"

"Hi," I say racking my brain for her name. Did she even give it to me? Shit. I don't remember.

"I take it you two went to the Bamboo Forest?"

"We did."

She smiles. "Sounds so romantic!"

I look at Logan. "Yeah. It was."

"Ughhhh, I can only imagine. You guys are seriously couple goals."

I'm glad we're outside in fading light. My cheeks are getting red, though to anyone else, they'd probably assume I'm thinking all sorts of naughty thoughts about Logan, not dealing with guilt and regret over the lie.

"I mean, the way he looks at you. Girl, you are so damn lucky! I'd give anything to have someone look at me like that."

I used to say that exact thing. *I'd give anything to have someone look at me like that*. And here we are…

"Time to go eat!" my sister calls. The bridesmaid whose name I can't remember hurries back to the group of girls, and I wait for Logan. He wraps his arm around my shoulder, and I can't tell if he's being genuine or if he's doing this for show right now.

We're eating at an open-air restaurant, with tables in the sand near the ocean. I take off my shoes and squish my toes in the sand under the table. We're seated at a table with a few other bridesmaids and groomsmen, and my parents are at a table right next to us. My father purposely takes a seat at the end of his table so he can talk to us, which was something I've been trying to avoid since I'm not the world's best liar.

We're all served red wine, and once we put in our order, I take Logan's hand and get up, saying we're going to walk along the water and take a few pictures. Diana, Peter, and another couple are down there, doing the same thing.

Logan takes my hand and we walk down to the water, going in ankle-deep. I get out my phone to take a few selfies.

"Want me to take a picture for you?" Diana asks, and I know it's her way of saying sorry for overreacting earlier. She's never been one to outright apologize.

"Yeah, that'd be great. Thanks." I hand her my phone and step back to Logan's side. He puts his arm around me, and we both smile.

"Do something cute," Diana tells us. "Kiss or something."

I look up at Logan, knowing that if we refuse to kiss, it'll be a dead giveaway that we're not really together. He knows it too, and I can see the *what the hell do we do* reflected in his eyes.

"Come on!" Diana giggles. "Kiss her already!"

Logan's lips part and his eyes lock with mine. This isn't the way our first kiss is supposed to happen—if it ever were to happen at all. It's not supposed to be forced or done for a show.

It's supposed to happen because I can't stand to go another minute without feeling his lips against mine.

But then he reaches forward, gently tucking my hair behind my ear. He trails his fingers down my cheek and down to my chin, tipping my face up to his. His hand around my waist pulls me closer, and I twist, turning my body toward his.

And then he kisses me.

CHAPTER 19

DANIELLE

Fireworks.

All I see are fireworks.

Waves crash against the shore, spraying our legs with water. A big one could sweep us out to sea, and I don't think I'd notice.

Because Logan Dawson is kissing me.

The second his lips touched mine, I knew we weren't acting anymore. Everything faded away, and right now, all I feel is him.

His lips against mine.

His arms around me.

His hips brushing against mine.

My heart is beating so fast I can feel my pulse throughout my entire body. Every nerve in my body tingles, and the heat that's rushing through me threatens to burn me from the inside out.

Logan slides his hand down my back, fingers resting right at the top of my ass. He moves his other hand from my chin to my hair, and my long locks tangle over his fingers. My lips part, welcoming his tongue into my mouth. Knees threatening to buckle, I reach up, needing to hold onto him for support.

Once my arms are around him, Logan pulls me in even closer, smashing my breasts against his chest. I grip him tight, holding him like my life depends on it. And right now, I suppose it does. Because I will wash out to sea if he stops kissing me.

Logan leans forward, bending me back as he slips his tongue into my mouth. A small whimper escapes my lips, making him kiss me even harder. He curls his fingers, taking a fistful of my hair.

I can taste the strawberry margaritas on both our lips, but kissing Logan is more intoxicating than any sort of alcohol.

Someone shouts something, maybe telling us to get a room? I'm not sure. Their voice is just a distant echo over my pounding heart. I push my hips up against Logan's, suddenly overtaken by desire. I feel Logan's cock through his pants, starting to harden against me. I sweep one hand down his shoulder, over his chest, and to his belt.

All the desire and emotion we've pent up over the year that we've been friends comes rushing out at a dizzying rate, and I want nothing more than to give in and give Logan everything.

Need for him swells inside me, and Logan starts to bunch up my dress with his fingers. I move my hand to the buckle on his belt, ready to undo it, pull it out of the belt loops, and unbutton his pants.

Suddenly, we both break apart at the same time, realizing how close we're coming to laying each other down right here in the sand, in front of my entire family and a few dozen strangers.

Holy.

Shit.

Logan just kissed me, and it was the best kiss I've ever had. The entire world faded around me in a way I never thought possible. That kiss was the thing romance novels center around. The subject of poems and love songs.

And if one kiss is that amazing, doing anything more…I don't know if I can handle it.

Breathless, I suck in air, blinking up at Logan. He's staring back at me with the same look in his eye, one that says *what the hell just happened* as well as *why the hell didn't we do that sooner?*

"I got a few good ones," Diana says, reminding me that she's here with us. Taking photos of Logan and me.

Of.

Our.

First.

Kiss.

"Th...thanks," I mumble, still not able to tear my eyes away from Logan. That's not the way I thought our first kiss would happen, but now that it did, I can't see it playing out any other way.

Logan moves his hand from the back of my head to my arm, gently running his fingers over my flesh and making goosebumps break out along my arm. He pulls me close once more when I shiver, and his body is so warm, so welcoming. It feels so right. I don't want to move away.

"Oh, appetizers are here!" Diana extends the phone to me, but I still can't move. Logan keeps one arm around me and reaches forward, taking my phone. We need to go to the table and eat, acting like everything is normal.

Like we kiss all the time.

Which we would, if we were really engaged.

Blinking, I tear my eyes away from Logan. We're not that far from the table, and the smell of food wafts through the air. I'm starving and not hungry at the same time. Another wave, bigger than the others, comes to shore, spraying us with water. Logan drops his hand from my body, and I miss his touch immediately.

"We should go eat," he says, voice somehow coming out strong and steady. I'm not sure I can string two words together and make a sentence right now. Everything inside me is running around, hands waving in the air and screaming with excitement.

Nothing has ever felt so right or natural than my lips connecting with Logan. Another surge of warmth goes through me when I think about connecting in other ways. I get wet just thinking about Logan on top of me, biceps flexed as he holds himself up. Lining his cock up to my core as I bend my legs and tilt my hips toward his.

"Danielle?"

I blink and realize I've been standing here holding my breath. It's just a kiss. I've been kissed before. I've had sex before. Lots of sex. So why do I feel like a virginal schoolgirl standing here before her crush?

Logan is doing bad, bad things to me…and I don't want him to stop. I know we need to go to the table and put on a different kind of act when we really need to talk about what just happened.

But mostly, I want him to kiss me again.

"Wait," I blurt and take his hand. My heart starts hammering again. What if that was just a fake kiss to him? What if he didn't react the same way I did? Physically, I know he enjoyed it, and my eyes flick to his cock of their own accord.

Logan moves his hand up, slipping his fingers through mine. "For what?"

"For you to kiss me again."

CHAPTER 20

LOGAN

She doesn't have to tell me twice. I rush forward, water splashing around my ankles, and wrap her in a tight embrace. Her arms go around my shoulders, and it's like our bodies were made to come together like this.

The moment my lips touch hers, I know I'm a goner. Kissing her harder than I did before, I don't know how we're going to stop. I've wanted to kiss Danielle since the first time I saw her. I've thought about it many times.

And this is better than anything I imagined.

I widen my legs and pull her closer, bending her back a bit as we kiss. My tongue goes in her mouth, and she slips one hand under my shirt, raking her nails over the skin on my back. Desire floods my veins, and I want nothing more than to pick her up and carry her back to our room.

"Hey, love birds!" someone shouts. "Time to eat!"

We should stop. Take a pause and come back to this. I'm still holding Danielle's phone and my grip is slipping. It's about to drop into the ocean, but I can't move away from Danielle.

Finally, we break apart, needing to get some air. I put Danielle's phone in my pocket before I accidentally drop it. My heart is racing, and I can't catch my breath to save my life. The wind picks up, blowing Danielle's damp hair around her face. I push it back and bring my lips to hers once more.

When I move away, she looks up at me and smiles. I'm not sure exactly what happened, but I know this isn't a game of pretend anymore. Not for me, and not for her.

"Now we really should go," I tell her.

"Right." She nods, looking at the table. Her arms are still around my neck, and she slowly drags them down, splaying her fingers over my chest. Her lips pull up into a smile. "I am really turned on right now."

"Me too."

She looks down at my semi-hard cock and bites her lip. Fuck, she's hot. "Yeah, I can tell. And that's making me even more turned on."

"Knowing you're getting even more turned on is turning me on even more."

We both laugh, and Danielle lets out a deep breath. "Logan…I…I…"

"Danielle!" her mother calls. "We need to say grace. Please come to the table!"

"We'll talk about it later." I take her hand and take a deep breath, slowly letting it out to try and calm myself down. I'm so revved up I can hardly stand it. I'm getting turned on all over again just by looking at Danielle.

I pull her chair out for her at the table and then go around, taking my seat across from her. Something needs to be said about what just happened…doesn't it? I can't seem to form a coherent thought, and suddenly everything I thought I knew about dating goes out the window.

If Danielle had been any other woman I'd been pursuing, a kiss would signal taking things to the next level, and we wouldn't sit down and discuss things until later on in the relationship when we were getting serious.

But Danielle and I are already serious, in a sense. She's my best friend, but I don't want to just be friends with benefits. I'm in love with her, and getting this close only to have her pull away will crush me.

Firelight from the tiki torches flickers over Danielle's face. Her cheeks are red, and the flush goes down her neck and over her chest. Seeing her physically react to the kiss is making me get hard again. I shift my weight in my chair and pick up my glass of water. I chug half of it.

Danielle serves the appetizers onto both our plates. A new glass of red wine was delivered with the appetizer, and she goes right for it, taking a few big drinks before shuddering.

"That is so dry."

Her face makes me laugh. "You drank half the glass before you realized that?"

"I swallowed it before I actually tasted it." She lets out a snort of laughter. "Sorry, that sounded dirty in my head."

"It kind of does sound dirty, which isn't helping my situation right now."

She squirms on her chair. "Mine neither." She takes another drink of wine, and I catch her hand after she puts the glass down.

"Danielle," I start, set on telling her the kiss means more to me than giving into physical needs.

"So, Logan," her dad butts in, scooting his chair out a bit. "Tell me about this bar you own. Danielle says it's profitable?"

Profits? What are profits? All I can think about right now are Danielle's beautiful eyes and the way she makes me feel whenever we're together.

"Dad," Danielle says, seeming just as flustered. "Can we not drill Logan right now?" She brings her wine to her lips again.

"When would be a good time to drill him?"

She chokes on the wine. Coughing, she wipes her mouth with her napkin and sets the glass down.

"Twenty-eight years old, and you still don't know how to

handle liquids," I quip, knowing she inhaled the wine because her mind went to the same place mine did. Well, assuming she was thinking a good time to drill me would be right fucking now.

Fuck. I'm going to have to dump my glass of ice water on myself soon.

Mr. Cross laughs. "All right. We can talk after dinner. No excuses this time, though."

"Yeah, that, uh, that's fine," Danielle stammers.

"The men are having a drink after dinner," Mr. Cross goes on. "Join us, and we can talk."

I nod. "Sounds good, Mr. Cross."

"Please, call me David. Or Dad," he adds with a wink. "But really don't."

"I'm sorry." Danielle goes for her water this time, taking a big drink.

"It's fine," I tell her. "It's expected since we're…we're getting married." The words have never sounded more contrived as they do right now. Something beautiful is starting between us, and talking like the beginning already happened seems wrong.

The couple next to us asks us about wedding dates and plans, and Danielle does her best to sidestep everything by saying we're in no rush and don't want anything big or fancy anyway.

Which is true.

Weston's first wedding was pretty typical, I'd say. Dean and Kara's was a bit extra because of Kara, and Quinn and Archer got married in Disney World. Wes and Scarlet's wedding was more my style, something small with close family and friends. But if Danielle did want a big wedding, I'd—wait.

We just kissed for the first time a few minutes ago.

Now I'm reaching for my wine.

The rest of the night goes by in a similar fashion, and it's so fucking weird to go from pretending to be a happy engaged couple who kiss and fuck and fight and make up all the time to pretending to be the same while ignoring the fact we finally kissed.

After dinner, Diana—who's a little drunk—grabs Danielle's arm and tells her she has to go to the bar near the pool and have a drink with her, celebrating her last night as a "single lady".

"I don't feel like drinking," Danielle tells her sister.

Diana dramatically gasps. "Are you pregnant?"

Danielle rolls her eyes. "I've been drinking all night, and not drinking doesn't mean someone is pregnant. That conclusion annoys me, actually."

"Well, by the way you two were all over each other, I wouldn't be surprised," Diana laughs.

Danielle gently pulls her arms from her sister's grasp. "Go get a drink and enjoy the night. We...we, uh, want to be all over each other again." Danielle cringes as she talks, and I'm feeling the pressure even more to tell her this isn't just some sort of no-strings hook-up. I don't want her thinking that's what I see this as.

I love her.

"Come on," Diana pesters. "Just have one drink. And isn't Logan having drinks with Dad and Peter? We're all going to be family soon anyway."

"It's okay," I tell Danielle, knowing part of her hesitation was so I wouldn't have to suffer through fake conversation with her father.

"Fine. One drink," Danielle tells Diana. She looks at me, and I can't help but smile, feeling heat flood my veins, tingling the tip of my cock. *Dammit.* "And I'll call you when we're done, and we can meet back up."

Diana pulls Danielle out of her seat, looping her arm through hers and leading her away from the table.

"Logan," Peter calls as Danielle walks away. "You're joining us, right?"

"Yeah. I am."

~

I SIT BACK, SWIRLING WHISKEY AROUND MY GLASS BEFORE TAKING A drink. Never in my life did I think I could be sitting outside at a bar along the ocean, drinking top-shelf whiskey that I'm not even paying for, and want to leave.

For the last twenty minutes, David and Peter's father have been complaining about how a country club back in Connecticut takes "any kind of people" nowadays "as long as they pay." I've considered breaking my glass and using the shards to gouge my eyes out just so I can have a legitimate reason to leave this conversation, but then my mother's voice rang loud in my head.

Country clubs and Ivy League schools are their thing. And that's okay. I shouldn't chastise them for having different interests as me. But this white-collar, keeping-up-with-the-Jones thing isn't me.

And it isn't Danielle either.

"Logan," David starts, setting his glass on the bar top. He's a man used to intimidating people, I can tell. It'll piss him off when that shit doesn't work on me. "We don't know each other well yet, but we do have one thing in common."

"We both care about Danielle and want her to be happy," I supply, and he nods.

"Right you are. She's my little girl, no matter how old she gets. You understand that, right?"

"I do. Making Danielle happy makes me happy."

"Good, good." He claps me on the back. "She's smart and has so much potential. You might be the last one who can convince her to go back to grad school. Between you and me, I'll be able to get her into a top-notch internship that will set her up for life."

I shake my head. "Danielle doesn't want to go back to grad school."

"Of course she does! Grad school is hard, trust me, I know." He looks at the others sitting around us and laughs, making sure everyone knows *he* went to grad school. "But the payoff is worth it. She'll thank you when she has a good job."

"I disagree."

Everyone in our party stiffens.

"You disagree?"

"Danielle doesn't want to go back to grad school," I repeat. "She told me she doesn't want to."

"You haven't known my daughter that long. Grad school has always been part of the plan. She'll regret it if she doesn't go. She needs it to get a good job and be successful."

"She doesn't think so."

David slowly shakes his head. He's not used to be questioned, and it's taken him aback. "A good education, a solid, respectable job…how can you argue against that? It was our ten-year plan and the thing Danielle has wanted her whole life. She's going through something, which is common, but she *will* regret it if she doesn't get back on track and out of that town."

"Have you even asked her what makes her happy?" I finish my whiskey and set the glass on the bar. "It's not grad school or fancy jobs." I lean toward David. "You say she's *going through something,* but have you ever stopped to consider the pressure you put on her to follow a life she doesn't want to live is the cause of all of that?"

"I…she…how dare you speak to me like that."

Out of respect for Diana and Peter—though I don't think that asshole deserves any—I leave it at that and get up and walk away before my temper gets the best of me. I don't really know where I'm going, but I keep walking until I'm back in the lobby of the hotel. Stopping to get my phone from my pocket, I realize I still have Danielle's phone too. Fuck. I don't know where she went with her sister. Assuming they stayed at the resort, I head through the lobby to check out another bar.

Her sister is there, but Danielle isn't. Diana thinks Danielle left to look for me, which means we probably just missed each other. This resort is huge, and each bar is on different ends. If I walk back, there's a chance we'll miss each other all over again.

I hang around the tiki bar with the bridesmaids for a bit, waiting to see if Danielle comes back. Ten minutes later, I head out to look for her, feeling drawn to the water for some reason.

I'm halfway to the other bar, walking outside, when I look out at the water. Danielle is standing on the shore, long hair blowing in the breeze behind her.

"Danielle," I say, coming up behind her. She turns, and a smile breaks out on her face. I can't get to her fast enough.

"Hey," she says, turning. Her arms are crossed tightly over her chest, and goosebumps cover her arms. There's a good chance things will be weird now that the moment has come and past.

"Are you cold?"

"Just a little chilled."

I wrap my arms around her, pulling her close to my body. "Does this help?"

"Yeah, it does. Thank you." She shuffles closer, resting her head against my chest. My eyes fall shut, and I rest my head against hers.

"I have your phone. I didn't realize I still did until I went to call you."

"I remembered after I frantically looked in my purse for it." Her arms are pulled in, sandwiched between her body and mine, trying to stay warm.

"How are you cold?" I ask with a laugh. "It's still hot outside."

"The breeze coming in over the ocean is cool, but I like watching the waves at night. It's hypnotic."

"It is." I run my hands up and down her arms, warming up her skin. Then I take her hand, lead her away from the damp sand, and sit on the beach. She sits between my legs, with her back to my chest. I wrap my arms around her, and she leans back, resting her head against me.

"This is nice," she says quietly, tipping her head up to mine.

It's better than nice. It's perfect. Running my fingertips along her arm, I look down at her pretty face.

"The ocean's so big." Her voice is quiet, and her eyes are set on the dark water. "I know that sounds like an obvious statement, but when you think about it, it's almost hard to fathom. It's so big across and then so deep at the same time. It's weird to think how we're just up here on the surface and so much is going on deep below, isn't it?"

"I've never really thought about it like that, but yeah, it is. There's so much unknown in the ocean."

"Right! That's why it freaks me out," she says with a laugh. "But I do kind of wish we had time to go snorkeling. Seems pretty safe."

"I think so. We'll add it to the list of things we want to do when we come back."

She puts her hand over mine. "I'd like that."

"Maybe we should just stay. Extend our vacation another week."

"Or two." She twists in my arms, looking into my eyes. "Can you imagine the fit Owen would throw if he found out we decided to just stay here a bit longer?"

I laugh. "I can because I've seen him throw a fit like that. And now staying is even more tempting." I bring my head down, unable to help myself any longer. My lips got to her neck, and a soft moan escapes Danielle's lips.

"It's really…tempting."

"Should we resist temptation?"

She spins in my arms, breaking out of my embrace. Brows furrowing, she locks eyes with me. I swallow hard, heart in my throat. We shared one epic kiss earlier, and I refuse to let that be our one and only. Each kiss will be better than the last.

My hands settle on her waist, directing her back to me. I straighten my legs and urge her forward. Danielle's breath leaves in a huff as she straddles me, dress bunching up around her tight little ass.

Cock jumping from the feel of her on top of me, I push her hair back and cup her face in my hands.

"No," she breathes. "We shouldn't resist it."

CHAPTER 21

DANIELLE

Everything hums inside of me. Every nerve in my body. Every inch of flesh. I'm straddling Logan, feeling his cock harden against me. I rock my hips, and just the fabric of his pants rubbing against me sends a jolt through me.

My face is cupped by both his large hands, and when he inches those long fingers along my cheek, I can't help but quiver. Because I know without a doubt those long fingers are going to be exploring more of my body tonight.

"Logan," I breathe, but don't get any more words out. He puts his mouth to mine and moves his hand to the back of my head, taking a tangle of hair in his grasp. I widen my legs, pressing myself down against his lap. His cock is getting harder, and—holy shit—it feels huge.

He brings his hands down to my hips, gripping me tight and pushing me down against himself. Then he angles his hips up, rubbing his hard cock against me. *Fuck!* I toss my head back, nails digging into his back. I'm getting wet already, and I swear he could make me come like this, rubbing against me through my panties.

I'm straddling Logan. Feeling his hard cock press against me. In the back of my mind, I know this could be a terrible idea.

He's my best friend. The one person in the world I know I can always count on. I should stop. Break away and get up.

Because sex can complicate things, and I don't want to ruin what we have.

He pushes my hair over my shoulder and puts his lips to my neck, kissing and sucking at my skin with fury. It sends a jolt to me, making me even wetter than I already was. His desperation makes mine worse, and now all self-control has gone out the window.

My lips part, and if I weren't kneeling in the sand, my legs would buckle and give out. Letting his hand fall down over my shoulder, he grabs one of my breasts through my dress. I'm not wearing a bra, and his fingers circle my pert nipple. I rock my hips again, rubbing myself against him.

"You are so fucking beautiful," he says between kisses, pinching my nipple between his index finger and thumb. I pitch forward, pussy so wet and so hot I need to come before I explode. His fingers go to the zipper on the back of my dress, and I put one hand on his cheek, kissing him with fervor.

He starts to undo my zipper, and my hands fall to his pants, fumbling with his belt. I get it unbuckled, and he starts to inch down the zipper.

"Danielle," he pants, breaking away.

Having his lips not on mine is like not breathing. Why the hell did he stop?

"Let's go to our room."

Room? What room? Oh shit, right. We're on the beach. A public beach. I blink, looking behind Logan at the glowing lights of our resort.

"I…I forgot where we were," I admit, inhaling deep. Logan pulls the zipper back up, but I don't have that kind of self-control. My hands are still on his cock, feeling the length and girth through his pants.

I don't know if that thing is going to fit inside of me. It if does, it might destroy me in the best way possible.

"There's no one out here," I groan.

"Fuck me." Logan puts his mouth to mine, unable to resist any longer. In a swift movement, he flips us over and moves between my legs.

"I plan to," I whisper as I go to kiss him again. His tongue pushes inside my mouth, and my pussy contracts. I want to push his head down and feel that tongue against my clit.

Voices echo along the beach. We stop kissing, but Logan makes no attempt to move off of me, and I'm still wrapped all around him. Separating will be physically impossible.

Swallowing hard, Logan starts to sit up. I don't want to stop because what if the moment is over? I'm so wound up and turned on it's going to take a lot to ruin the moment though.

Logan gets up and extends a hand for me. Sand falls off me, and Logan laces his fingers through mine. Licking my lips, I look down at his cock, which is so big and so hard it's barely contained by his pants.

I mean to tell him that I'll walk in front of him and we'll go straight to our room. But it comes out as, "I want you," which doesn't help our situation at all. Hand in hand, we rush into the hotel. The elevator is crowded, and standing here, smashed up against Logan and his monster dick, I start to think about what we almost did.

And how much I want to do it.

We get into the room, and with anyone else, the vibe would be gone and things would be a little weird. But it's not.

Not at all.

Logan's arms go around me as soon as the door shuts, and it's like we never stopped. Pushing me up against the door, he gathers my dress up in one hand while kissing my neck. I slit my eyes open as I wrap my arms around him.

My heart is racing and my breath hitches. Logan's hands are on me. One is edging dangerously close to my core, and I almost can't believe this is happening.

Finally happening.

He pushes his hips against mine, pinning me against the door. His cock presses against me, making me weak. I bring my hand to his chest, dragging my fingers down until I get to the waistband of his pants. I circle the button, and suddenly Logan breaks away.

It's like someone ripped off my oxygen mask and now I can't breathe. My lips part, but I can't form any words. Right when I think he's realizing what we're doing, that this is crazy or stupid or maybe both, he looks at me with so much lust in his eyes I think I'm going to burst into flames.

"You are beautiful," he whispers again, inching his fingers between my legs. I willingly spread them for him, knowing he can feel the heat before his fingers even sweep over me. I let my head fall back against the door.

Logan brings his head down, resting his forehead against mine for a moment before kissing me hard again. It's an intimate gesture and one that throws me. Because as much as I'm turned on, as much as I need this physical release, it's so much more.

His tongue enters my mouth at the same time his hand plunges inside my panties.

"Fuck, you're wet," he groans, deft fingers circling my entrance. I hold onto him, struggling to stay upright on my feet. He's making my knees weak and my entire body quiver head to toe with desire.

"You're making me wet," I whisper back.

"What do you want me to do about it?" His breath is warm against my skin. I push myself against his hand. He knows what I want him to do.

"This," I groan.

"Tell me," he growls. "I want to hear you say it."

Holy shit. I never took Logan to be a commanding lover, and I'm not sure I can handle it. I need to have him inside me. Now.

"I want you to fuck me, Logan. I want your fingers inside me. I want your mouth all over me. And then I want your cock."

"*Fuuuuck*," he moans, and his mouth goes to my neck again. He widens my legs and sweeps his fingers over my clit. A jolt of pleasure goes through me, and I grip him tighter to keep from falling. He's taking his time, teasing me, knowing he's driving me absolutely wild.

Finally, he slips a finger inside of me, giving me a taste of what's to come. Then he pulls his hand back, yanks my panties down, and drops to his knees. My mouth falls open, and I press myself against the wall, looking down at him.

He's balling my dress back up in one hand and brings the other to the back of my thigh. My eyes close and he puts his mouth to me, kissing my inner thigh before turning his head up, warm breath against my pussy.

He kisses his way up my stomach, stopping only so he can undo the zipper of my dress. He gets back to his feet and pulls the zipper all the way down. Stepping back, he watches the dress fall to the floor and I'm left standing there, completely naked, in front of Logan.

And now he's looking at me like I'm the only woman in the world, like if he doesn't put his body against mine, he won't live to see another day. He runs his eyes over me, admiring every single inch of my body.

I've struggled with my body image my whole life. Some days I'm okay with how I look. And some days all I see are my flaws when I look in the mirror. My stomach isn't flat. I have cellulite on my thighs. One of my breasts sits a little higher up than the other.

"You are so fucking hot," he growls as if my flaws don't exist at all. I drop my eyes to his cock again, straining against his pants. Logan steps in close, hands landing on the curve of my hips. He brings them down over my ass, giving it a squeeze before picking me up and carrying me to the bed.

We fall onto the mattress together, and I scramble to get Logan's pants undone. I pop the button, and his big cock forces the zipper down. The tip is sticking out past the elastic of his boxers, and I swirl my fingers over the wet tip. Logan groans, melting against me as I stroke him. But right as I push my hand inside and wrap my fingers around his thick shaft, he grabs my wrist and pulls my hand out.

"Don't you want me to—"

He shuts me up with a kiss, pinning my arms up above me. My body hums with anticipation, and he starts to kiss his way down. He looks up at me right before he takes my breast in his mouth, and the half-second glance is all I need.

Because in that half-second, I see the same look in Logan's eyes than I did the first time we ever met. The longing for something he didn't know he wanted…for the one thing that fills his heart.

It's me.

His tongue flicks over my nipple, and I shut my eyes, bringing one hand up and tangling my fingers in his hair. Logan trails kisses down over my stomach. He parts my legs, and I suck in a breath, body shaking. He puts his lips to my thigh, gently kissing my skin. He's moving closer and closer, getting me so wound up by his slow teasing. I push myself up on my elbow, gripping the tangle of hair tighter in my hand. If I have to guide his head to my pussy, I will.

Because I need him so fucking bad right now.

Logan turns his head, and his nose brushes over my clit. Opening his mouth, he kisses my other thigh, but he's not as gentle this time. He sucks hard, nipping my skin with his teeth. The change in sensation makes me gasp, and it's taking all the self-control in the world right now not to lie back and put my own hand between my legs right now, stroking my clit until I come hard against my own hand.

It wouldn't take me long. Logan has already gotten me so worked up I could come in under a minute.

"I...I need you," I pant, hands shaking as I try to urge him to my core. Logan slips his hands under my ass, lifting my hips off the mattress. One leg goes over his shoulder, and he looks right into my eyes before diving back down. The stubble on his cheeks rubs against me, and he puts his open mouth on me, tongue lashing my clit.

Holy. Fucking. Shit.

His mouth is warm. Wet. *Skilled*. No one has ever done to me what he's doing with that tongue right now, and my eyes roll back in my head as the orgasm builds. I was close to coming before he even started, and now I know it's not going to take long.

He holds my tender core against him as he eats me out, and my breath starts to come out in ragged huffs. My muscles contract as my body prepares for the climax. I'm right there, teetering on the edge.

And then Logan stops.

He turns his head to my thigh again, leaving me reeling. My mouth falls open, and my pussy contracts, but the orgasm never comes.

"Please," I beg, feeling like I'm going to implode. Heat is building up inside me. "Oh, God, Logan, please!"

He reaches down, taking a hold of his cock, and he looks at me, knowing he's got me right where he wants me. Stroking himself, he licks his lips.

"If you won't, I will," I threaten but can hardly bring my hand up because everything inside of me is jittering with need.

"I do like to watch," he says, and I don't know how his voice is coming out so level and even right now. Wide-eyed, I look at him, and my heart hammers even faster. "But I do love the way you taste." Then he dives back down, mouth going to my core. He licks, sucks, and kisses me, moving his tongue in a fast circle around my clit.

My legs go over his shoulders, and he lifts my hips off the mattress again. His head is buried between my legs, holding me as close to him as possible. His tongue lashes out once more, and the orgasm that was building erupts like a storm. My pussy spasms and I try to move away as I'm overcome and so fucking sensitive right now.

He doesn't relent and keeps his mouth against me, working that magic tongue. He lowers me back onto the mattress and slips a finger inside me, going right to my G-spot. My pussy is still spasming wildly from the first orgasm, and a second hits me, catching me off guard.

Wetness spills from me, soaking his face and hand. Logan groans, turned on by feeling me come like this. No one has made me come this hard before. I've done it myself a time or two with my vibrator, and I was certain no man could get me off this much.

But, fuck, I was wrong.

My entire body is alive, and I'm squirming against Logan, ears ringing and stars dotting my vision. Logan lays me down and wipes his face with the back of his hand.

"Should I be sorry?" I pant, feeling the aftershock of the orgasm pulse through me.

"Hell no. Seeing you come that hard is so hot," he says, moving next to me. He's still fully clothed, and while my body is still riding high, not yet able to come down, I know we're far from being done.

Because Logan Dawson has yet to fuck me.

"No one has made me do that before," I admit, reaching for him. My hands are still shaking, and I don't think I could get up and walk if I tried. Heart hammering, I turn toward Logan and look into his eyes.

"Take your shirt off," I tell him, and he flashes a cocky grin, sitting up on the mattress. Light from the balcony doors spills in, illuminating his muscular body as he pulls his shirt over his head. Then he falls back onto me, and I widen my legs. I taste myself on his lips as we kiss, and I feebly push his pants and boxers down, stripping him naked.

Logan is trying to be patient, trying to give me a minute to recover. I bend my legs up and the glistening tip of his cock rubs over me. He lets out a groan, burying his face against my neck.

"Danielle," he growls, and then it's like he can't wait any longer. I'm getting worked up all over again, and while we're moving fast, both desperate for a release, there's something tender in his touch, something that's so magnetic and feels so right. It's more than just two people meeting a physical need.

It's like we were made for this. Like we were meant to be together.

Logan brings his face back to mine, kissing me as he lines his cock up to my entrance. I widen my legs and angle my hips up, heart in my throat. He kisses me hard and pushes that big dick inside of me, filling every single inch.

I cry out in pleasure, body going into overdrive. I'm still so hot and worked up from before. My clit is sensitive, and just having his thick cock inside of me rubs my G-spot in the perfect way.

I know I'll be coming again, which is another thing no one has ever made me do.

Logan starts off slow, drilling his cock in and pulling it out until only the tip remains. It hits me in the sweet spot, and I shudder, muscles tensing as another orgasm builds inside. He pushes in and pulls back again, breath coming out in a huff.

Then he gives in, unable to hold out anymore, and starts fucking me hard and fast. My mouth falls open, and I grip him tight, digging my nails into the skin on his back. He lowers himself against me and slips one arm under my body. His movements slow, but then he flips us over, pulling me on top

Gasping, I reposition us and plant my hands on his chest, riding him hard. He holds my hips, grinding me against him. I come again, leaning forward with my breasts in Logan's face. His fingers press into my skin as he comes, bucking his hips up. I feel his cock pulsing, filling me.

I collapse onto Logan, hands trembling as I gulp in air. Gently, Logan moves us, pulling out and spooning his body around mine.

"No one has ever made me come that way before either," I confess as Logan pulls the sheet over us.

"Yeah, I'm good." He pulls me close.

I smile, snuggling a little close to Logan.

He is good.

We are good.

Good friends...and even better lovers.

CHAPTER 22

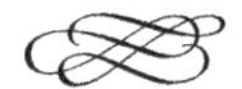

DANIELLE

I roll over, stretching my arms out. In his sleep, Logan reaches for me, and I move back into his embrace, nuzzling against his chest. Muted sunlight streams through the open balcony doors. My hair is a tangled mess around my face. I'm thirsty and have to pee, but I've never been more comfortable than I am right now, lying under twisted sheets with Logan.

It's like our bodies were meant to be together.

My heart is so full, and for the first time in my life, things feel like they're going exactly the way they're supposed to. That all the things I thought were mistakes were actually mile markers. The road was twisted, uphill, and slippery most of the way, but it led to me being exactly where I'm supposed to be.

Right here with Logan.

My best friend.

And the man I love.

Grumbling to myself, I tear away from Logan's arms and get up, stumbling to the bathroom to pee and get a drink. Then I fall back onto the mattress, and Logan spoons his body around mine. I'd only slept maybe an hour before waking up, and I roll over, pushing Logan down onto the mattress.

I'm so fucking tired, but I can't help the desire that's taking me over. The warmth starts between my legs, wetting my pussy. It spreads upward through my stomach, filling me with the need to have Logan's tongue...fingers...cock...preferably all three, on me.

In me.

"Are you awake?" I whisper, hooking my leg over Logan's.

"Yeah," he mumbles. "You...you okay?"

"I want you." That gets his attention. "But if you're too tired for a quickie, I understand."

"I will never be too tired for you, Danielle." He pulls me onto him and runs his hands up the back of my thighs, squeezing my butt cheeks. It's like now that we started, we can't stop even though we both know we should sleep.

But I'm hot and wet and need this.

So does Logan.

He flips me over, and puts his hand between my thighs, slowly raking his fingers over my skin. I groan and widen my legs.

"You're not very patient, are you?" Logan growls and sweeps his fingers up over my clit. I open my mouth to tell him I've been patient, that I've wanted this since pretty much the first time I saw him. But all that comes out is a moan, and he pushes one of his long fingers inside me.

I'm lying on my back with Logan at my side. I'm not really at a good angle to reach out and stroke him at the same time, and knowing how good he's going to give it to me is making me a selfish lover already.

My body revs up with anticipation, and he goes back and forth from rubbing my G-spot to my clit, getting me worked up hard and fast. The orgasm is building up in me, and my breath hitches in my chest. I bring one hand up, digging my fingers into Logan's arm as I come, pussy spasming around his fingers.

Ears ringing, I feebly pull him to me, spreading my legs and welcoming him in between. He kisses my neck, having already figured out what being kissed in that spot does to me. I wrap my arms around his muscular torso right as he pushes inside, driving his cock in and out of me slowly at first before he picks up the pace. He's at the perfect angle, and I'm already so fucking turned on. Another orgasm rolls through me, and feeling my pussy tighten around his cock sends Logan over the edge.

He pushes in balls deep as he comes, letting his head drop and rest against mine. We're both panting, and my heart is racing. Butterflies are still flapping around in my stomach, and I don't want this feeling to ever go away.

"I came inside you," Logan breathes, slowly pulling out. "A few times now. I, uh, didn't even think about it."

"I make you get carried away, I know. I would say it's a curse if it didn't benefit me just as much."

"That sounds like a good problem to have," Logan laughs and reaches over for the box of tissues on the nightstand, pulling a few out and handing them to me.

"I know, right? But yeah…about that. I'm on the pill. I have been since I was like fourteen. Painful periods."

"Oh, right. I remember you mentioning that now. In detail."

"You're my best friend. You get the nitty gritty of my life." Smiling, I get out of bed as gracefully as I can for someone who's trying to discretely wipe themselves clean. I clean myself up and get back into bed, falling right into Logan's arms. A warm breeze blows through the open door, and Logan's strong arms wrap tight around me.

Life is perfect.

"DANIELLE."

"Hmmm," I grumble. It's physically impossible for me to open my eyes right now. I can feel sunlight streaming through the

windows and door. If I weren't half asleep, I'd get up and close the blinds.

"Dani." Logan's lips brush over my ear as he speaks. It's not fair for him to turn me on this much while I'm exhausted. "Your alarm has been going off. I hit snooze twice for you already."

His words should shock me, but I'm way too tired to care right now. I'm just too comfy in his arms, snuggled under soft sheets. If I thought the waterfalls were paradise, I was sadly mistaken. *This* is paradise, right here, naked and half asleep, in Logan's arms.

"Danielle," he repeats, gently tucking my hair out of my face. "Today is your sister's wedding. It's nine-thirty already."

This time his words do shock me. "Fuck." I sit up, eyes flying open.

"I take it I shouldn't have hit snooze?"

"It's not your fault." I rub my forehead, wanting nothing more than to go back to sleep in Logan's embrace. "I have a salon appointment at ten."

"You have time still." He snakes an arm around me. "And we both know I don't need much time to make you come so hard you leave a puddle on the sheets."

"Dammit, Logan," I groan and flop back onto the mattress. My stomach gets all fluttery and my core quivers, begging me to lie back and let him pleasure me. "I have to shower and shave and then try to dry my hair before getting to the salon."

He's already moved over the top of me. And his cock is hard. The tip gleaming with pre-cum. *Fuck.* Biting my lip, I close my eyes and reach down, wrapping my fingers around his thick cock. I bring the tip against my clit and slowly circle my hips.

We're making up for lost time, that's for sure. I've never had this much sex in this short a time in my entire life.

"You are so fucking hot," Logan groans, burying his face in my neck. He kisses my skin, and my own eyes flutter shut. I arch my hips and slowly start moving them in small circles.

My breath comes out in a huff, and Logan moves to the side, reaching down and finishing what I started. I come against his fingers, writhing in pleasure on the mattress. My pussy is still spasming when he climbs back on top and pushes that big dick inside of me.

My mouth falls open, and stars dot my vision. He thrusts all the way inside of me, groaning as he buries his cock in deep. I can feel my pussy contract around his cock, and I angle my hips up, getting hit at a different angle. He bucks his hips hard and fast, rocking me into oblivion. I come for the second time, and only a few seconds later, he comes too, filling me with everything he has.

Resting his forehead against mine, he kisses me softly as he waits for his cock to stop pulsing. I don't know how I'm going to get up and function. Not only has Logan destroyed me physically with his big dick, I'm exhausted and spoiled and don't want to do anything other than lie here and make love to him.

"Should I be sorry?"

"Hell no," I pant. "But you should help me shower. Wait, no. I need to take a fast shower, and I'm suddenly incapable of being naked around you without it turning into sex."

"Your problems just keep adding up."

I laugh and get out of bed, taking a quick shower. I wrap up in a towel and brush through my wet hair, looking at the time on my phone. I have ten minutes to get down to the salon, and it takes me at least fifteen to dry my hair when it's this sopping wet.

I do the best I can and go back into the room to get dressed in record time. Logan is back in bed, half-covered with the blankets and looking so comfortable it's not fair.

"Want me to bring you breakfast or coffee?"

"If there's nothing at the salon, hell yes. Usually, someone brings coffee and bagels or donuts to something like this. Though I wouldn't be surprised if Diana brings kale and sugar-free tea," I tell him, pulling a pair of underwear on. I let the towel drop and try to hide my smile when I see Logan's reaction to my body. There's something rather empowering about being able to turn a man on like this.

It's even better when it's one you're head over heels in love with.

I put my bra on next and then yank a tank top on over my head. "Shit," I swear when I pick up my phone. I forgot to charge it last night, and it's at one percent. I stick it and the charger in my purse. I'll be able to charge it at the salon, I'm sure.

I put on a skirt, step into my shoes, and go over to the bed, kissing Logan goodbye before hurrying out the hotel room and to the salon. I'm just a few minutes late when I walk through the door, but the stylist isn't ready for me yet anyway.

My mother is all smiles today—as she should be—and gives me a hug when I walk into the back room. There are coffee and pastries, thank the stars. I pour myself a cup and grab a cinnamon bagel.

Diana comes into the back as I'm inhaling my coffee. Her makeup has been done already, and she looks beautiful.

"I'm not an emotional person," I start, setting the coffee down. "But I'm getting all teary-eyed, sis. You look like a princess already."

Diana looks up, doing whatever she can to keep her own eyes from watering. "Thank you. I can't believe I'm getting married today! In Hawaii!" She waves her hands around in the air as she squeals.

She's happy, which makes me happy. But, dammit, I still wish she were marrying a better man than Peter.

Yawning, I reach for my coffee and take another mouthful down.

"Up late?" Mom asks, picking up a bagel to cut in half.

"Yeah." I finish my coffee and go for a refill.

"What were you doing?" Diana asks with a giggle as she wiggles her eyebrows at me.

"I'm not at liberty to say." I pour more coffee into the paper cup.

Diana giggles again, and Mom rolls her eyes. "Oh come on, Mama," Diana starts. "We're adults. Dani's lived with boyfriends before."

"I still don't need to hear you talk about it. Unless you want me to talk about my night." Mom gives us a wink.

"Ew, please don't!" Diana laughs. Luckily, the stylist is ready for Mom, and she goes out of the backroom, leaving Diana and me alone.

"You seem happy," she says to me, looking at the donuts but not picking one up.

"You seem surprised by that."

"I am," she admits. "Just as surprised to find out you're engaged when you haven't so much as mentioned a boyfriend."

Shit. "I didn't want to admit to myself how serious it was," I say, which isn't actually a complete lie. "I went to Eastwood with the assumption I'd leave." I flick my eyes to Diana, knowing this is a sore subject. Whatever, though, right? She chose to forgive Peter, to believe his lies over the truth.

But I'm sure she knows.

And I know I wasn't the first woman he made a move on while he and Diana were together. All I can hope now is that he's grown up, and proposing and wanting to get married right after I called him out was a wakeup call of some sorts, making him realize what he had to lose or something like that.

"So why start a serious relationship when you'd just take off again?" Diana supplies, doing a nice job of slipping in a backhanded insult.

"Right. But Logan is…" I trail off, smiling. "He's everything I could ever want."

"So, you're going to stay in that little town?"

"I like it there, and I don't know why that's so hard to believe. It's not like it's some backwoods town down south or something.

We're about two hours from Chicago, we have two Starbucks now, and Papa John's just started delivering. Plus, there's a new big hospital being built, and there's talk of an Olive Garden going in nearby."

"Sounds…charming."

"Grandpa wasn't wrong picking that place to lay down roots. It's not your thing, and that's okay."

"I just don't see how you can't like the finer things in life." She's not trying to be mean. Diana really can't understand how anyone can differ from her and not be miserable.

"It was too much pressure. Too much bullshit and everyone was fake. But that's your thing," I add, realizing it's a little too late to circle back around and not insult her. I don't know what Diana actually does right now. She's not book smart, but that doesn't make her stupid, though according to our father, it did, and she grew up knowing she didn't have what it takes to get into the Ivies.

What the fuck? Am I actually starting to empathize with my bitchy sister? I sip my coffee and watch her smiling down at her ring. Being a housewife to a "successful man" was never something I wanted.

I wanted to be the successful person my parents wanted me to marry. I might not be there just yet, but I'm on my way.

CHAPTER 23

LOGAN

I wasn't prepared for this. It was the last thing I thought would happen, but it did. And now I can't stop smiling when I look at Danielle. She's standing up for her sister, holding a bouquet of brightly colored flowers. Her hair is pulled back in a loose bun at the nape of her neck, and she looks absolutely beautiful.

This is the longest I've seen her since she left this morning to get her hair done. Things ran over at the salon, and she had to run back to the room, change, and then head down to the beach with the rest of the bridal party for photos. I'm sitting in the back, and I don't know a single person around me. Though even if I did, it wouldn't matter.

My eyes are on Danielle and Danielle alone, as they will be the rest of the night.

Things are fucking perfect right now, and as soon as we get time together at the reception, I'm going to pull her aside and tell her everything.

This wasn't some vacation hookup.

I don't want to be fuck buddies, even though we're really good at fucking.

I am in love with her, and I want to tell her how I feel just as much as I want to make love to her again. The sun is beating down on us, but the breeze makes sitting outside in dress clothes manageable. Danielle catches my eye and smiles. My cock jumps, thinking about her last night.

And this morning.

And then again this morning.

She's so fucking hot, and my mind starts to drift to her body on mine, to the way her pert nipples feel against my tongue. To her tight, wet pussy.

I look away, shifting my eyes to the ocean behind Danielle. The ceremony cannot end fast enough. Time seems to drag on, and I'm sweating by the time we finally stand to receive the bride and groom.

Everyone heads inside for a cocktail hour before the actual reception starts, and I find Danielle in the hall waiting for me. She's still holding her flowers and wraps her arms around my neck as soon as we're close.

Why the hell did I wait so fucking long to make a move? Nothing has ever felt more natural than having Danielle in my arms like this.

"Want to get a drink?" she asks, standing on her toes to kiss me.

"I take it you do?" My hands settle on her waist, and I bring her hips in against mine.

"Yes, it was hot standing there, and I think my shoulders got sunburned. I didn't think about putting sunscreen on." She wrinkles her nose.

"Your shoulders do look a little red."

"Dammit. Maybe you can be super sexy later and rub aloe on it for me."

"I like when you talk dirty to me." I push one hand over her hip and to her ass, giving it a squeeze. She brings one hand up and runs her fingers through my hair. My eyes shut in a long blink, and I tip my head down, resting my forehead against hers.

"What are you thinking about?" she asks as she continues to bring her hand down until her fingers hover over the zipper on my pants. She knows what I'm thinking about. She can feel it.

"I'm thinking about," I start, and bring my lips to her ear, "taking you upstairs and unzipping your dress. Watching it fall and then laying you down on the bed. I'm going to take my time with you, Danielle, licking and sucking, and kissing your pussy until you're begging me to let you come."

"Fuuuck," she groans and curls her fingers under the waist of my pants.

"Are you getting wet?"

"Mm-hm," she whimpers. "I want you to stick your hand inside my panties and feel how wet you're making me."

"You're killing me, Danielle."

"Don't die yet." She inhales, breasts rising and falling beneath her dress. "I need you to slay me again later." Biting her lip, she looks up, cheeks starting to grow red. "Even though you already did. I could feel you between my legs hours after we made love. Every step reminding me of your big cock inside of me."

I bring my head up and look into Danielle's eyes. "Is there a coat closet we can sneak off to now?"

Danielle's lips curve into a smile. "We do have a hotel room a few floors up. I think we can sneak away and no one would notice."

A waiter comes around, handing out glasses of champagne. Danielle takes her hands off me, sets the flowers down on a table near us, and gets two glasses of champagne. She gets on small sip in before she's called away to be in more photos back outside on the beach. She downs her drink before going outside, and I grab a few appetizers, walking around to kill the time.

Right as Danielle comes back, everyone is ushered into the reception hall, and Danielle stays back with the bridal party so they can be introduced as they walk in. Danielle's a bridesmaid, but we're sitting together thankfully. There are way too many people in the bridal party for them all to fit at one head table.

There are more people here than I expected. At least double the number who were at Quinn and Archer's wedding, and that wasn't across an ocean. I entertain myself by people watching until Danielle comes in, looking uncomfortable as she walks over the dance floor. The guy she's walking with is Peter's brother, and he does some sort of dance move that's supposed to be funny but leaves me cringing just as much as Danielle.

She hefts into her seat when we get to the table, sinking down low.

"Cute," I tease, and she responds with a glare. The rest of the bridal party is introduced, and then we all stand and clap for the bride and groom. Danielle and I get another round of drinks before the food comes, which we thankfully don't have to wait long for.

"So I should probably introduce you to my grandma," Danielle tells me as she cuts into her food. "My dad's mom. She's kind of awful, and we were never really close. She said she already raised two kids and didn't want to be involved when Diana and I were young. Though meeting her does help you understand why my dad is the way he is. You might even feel like you should give him credit for not growing up a homicidal maniac."

"She can't be that bad."

Danielle nods her head. "Oh, she is. You know how your nana has no filter and just blurts things out all the time?"

"Yeah. It's always fun when Archer's around." I shake my head. Nana always hits on Archer, and it's hilarious and awkward at the same time.

"My grandma is like that, but she's one hundred percent with it. She just says the mean things she's thinking. But…"

"But she's family."

"Right. Speaking of, I called my grandpa after the ceremony and haven't heard back yet."

"He's probably playing Bingo or taking advantage of the empty house and invited more lady friends over."

"Gross!" she playfully nudges me. "But you're right."

"About the lady friends? I knew it."

"No, about him being out and about. Half the time he doesn't remember to bring his phone anywhere. Or if he does, he keeps it on silent and can't hear it ring."

"I'm guilty of that too," I remind her. The bar gets so loud I can't hear my phone ring anyway. "Is that your grandma?" I ask, pointing to an angry-looking older woman, talking to Danielle's dad.

"Yep. It's amazing how much that woman can complain."

"Some people are good at it."

"She's one of them, for sure."

The cake cutting comes next, followed by the first dance. Then the dance floor opens up, and Danielle looks at me with a smile.

"Dance with me?"

"I think I can manage that." It'll be a good chance to get her alone so I can tell her how I really feel.

We stop at the open bar first and get the "signature drink" of the night, which is something fruity and the same color as the wedding colors. I really don't get all the extra effort put into weddings like this. I guess it's neat and well thought out…but doesn't seem necessary to me.

Danielle's a little bit tipsy right now, but if there was any night to drink, it would be tonight, celebrating the wedding and everything that has happened between us. I feel like celebrating at least.

"Danielle," someone calls, and Danielle looks over, making a face. She's not very good at hiding her emotions as is, and is even worse when she's been drinking. It's fucking adorable.

"It's Grandma." Danielle takes another big gulp of her drink and puts on a fake smile, turning to give her grandmother a hug.

"Hi, Grandma, how are you?"

"Still getting used to this time change," her grandma replies, gently patting Danielle on the back. "And right when I get used to it, I'll go home to Hartford and have to get used to that time change all over again."

"Yeah, it's an adjustment."

"How's grad school treating you?"

"Grandma, you know I'm not going anymore. It wasn't for me," Danielle starts, having more patience than I would have.

"You know who says that? Quitters. And the Crosses aren't quitters."

Danielle takes another drink. "If anything, quitting was harder than going."

"What kind of crazy talk is that? Quitting is the easy way out."

Danielle just smiles and nods, going back to her drink. I know exactly what she means. Quitting meant finally veering off the path that had been laid out for her. It meant telling her father she wanted to do something different with her life.

Danielle's eyes are getting a little bloodshot. Over the years of tending and then owning a bar, it's easy to spot people who are getting close to their limits of what they can handle. Danielle's always cut herself off before she's gotten to that point, but with her family around…who knows? I place my hand on the small of her back. She doesn't have to worry about it tonight. I'll take care of her.

"Well, at least introduce me to this handsome fellow." Grandma Cross eyes me up and down. "At least you're doing something right, Dani."

"This is my friend, Logan," Danielle introduces. "And Logan—"

"Friend? Just a friend?" Grandma cross grabs Danielle's hand and brings it to her face. "That's not what I heard."

"R-right," Danielle stammers.

"What she means," I start, wrapping my arm around her, "is

that we were friends first and then started dating. She still is my friend, and now I can't wait for her to be my wife."

The closer I get to Danielle, the more I hate lying. Even after finally hooking up, the lies feel wrong, like it's cheapening what we have between us.

"Friendship is a good foundation to build a marriage on." Grandma Cross pats Danielle's arm. "Best of luck to the both of you, and Danielle, when you change your mind about grad school, you let me know. Some of the women in my gardening club have husbands in high places."

Danielle tries to fake a smile but can't hide the sour look on her face. She knows it too and covers it up by bringing her drink to her lips. She pokes herself in the face with her straw.

"Let's dance," I say, taking the drink out of her hand.

"You just want to put your hands on me." Her eyebrows go up.

"I do." I take a sip and then set the glasses down on a table, moving back to Danielle. Both hands land on her hips, and she leans up to kiss me. "I still think we should try to sneak out of here."

She nods, and then a song comes on that she likes. Grabbing my hand, she turns and drags me to the dance floor. We drink and dance, stealing kisses and copping feels just to make each other laugh.

When Danielle steps away to use the bathroom, I go back to our table to get a drink of water. I sit down and pull my phone out of my pocket. I'm surprised to see not one, but two missed calls from Weston. I don't remember the last time we actually spoke on the phone, and it was most likely Jackson, my nephew, calling to say hi and ask about Hawaii. The last call was from only seven minutes ago, so I call back.

"Hello?" Weston answers.

"Hey, Wes. Did Jackson call?"

"No, I did."

"Is everything okay? Jackson—"

"He's fine."

"Emma?"

"Fine too."

I lean back in the chair. "Then why are you calling?" Wes hates talking on the phone. He never calls. Hell, he rarely responds to the group text we've had going on for years with Owen and Dean.

"Are you with Danielle?"

"No, I came all the way to Hawaii, and we parted ways." I swallow hard. "Why?"

"Her grandpa," he starts. "He had a heart attack."

"Fuck. Is he…he's alive, right?"

"Yeah. I responded to the call, and he's at the hospital now. I was able to get a hold of the doctor, and he couldn't tell me much, but he said Danielle should come home. Now."

CHAPTER 24

DANIELLE

I look at myself in the mirror as I wash my hands, and for the first time in a long time, I don't pick apart my appearance. Having my hair and makeup professionally done helps, but mostly…I look happy.

Because I am.

So incredibly fucking happy, and nothing can dampen my mood. Want and desire swell inside of me, and I'm going to go find Logan and take him up to our room. He said he was going to take his time with me, but I want to do the same to him.

Tie him up. Tease him. Make *him* beg for more.

I dry my hands, smooth out my dress, and go back to the reception hall. Logan is at the table, with his back to me. A smile pulls up my lips, and no matter how hard I try, I can't stop smiling.

Logan turns around, almost like he can sense me coming. He's on the phone, and something isn't right.

"What's wrong?" I ask, rushing over to him.

"I'll call you back," Logan says to whoever he's talking to.

"Logan?" I'm getting a little freaked out. "What's wrong?"

"That was Wes," he starts and brings one hand up to the back of his neck.

"Oh my God. Is Jackson okay? Did Daisy come back?"

Logan shakes his head. "No, she didn't, and Jackson is fine. Wes responded to a call and…I'm so sorry." His brown eyes meet mine. "Your grandpa had a heart attack."

"What?" I shake my head. "No. He didn't. He's…he's fine."

Logan puts his hand on my arm, and I jerk away. I don't want comfort. Because comfort means something bad happened, and nothing bad happened.

There is no reason for comfort.

Logan and I are finally together. I realized who I am and how I'm on the path I'm supposed to be on.

Grandpa is fine.

"Wes told me the doctor says to come home right away. They're treating him now, but…but…they're not sure if he'll pull through," he says, struggling to say the words out loud. He puts his hand on me again, and this time I need it. I fall against him, still trying to process everything.

"What…what happened?"

"Wes said he collapsed during Bingo. Wes was on call and got there right as the paramedics did. He's at the hospital, but we should…we should go home."

"Now?"

"Yeah," he says, and what he *doesn't* say weighs down on me. There isn't much time, and I'm halfway around the world right now.

"I…I should tell my mom."

Logan takes my hand. "I'll come with you."

I blink back tears. "Thank you."

Logan stands and helps me to my feet. He cradles me to his chest, and I let my eyes fall shut. Alcohol floods my veins, and I wish I could puke it all out while at the same time want to down another drink. With my hand firmly in Logan's, we walk through the room, looking for my parents.

My mom is talking with Diana and Peter, smiling and laughing without a care in the world. Today is supposed to be a good day. A happy day. A carefree day of no worries and no stress.

"Danielle!" Mom says, looking my way. "You look so lovely this evening, my dear."

"Hey...can we talk?" Logan starts, eyes darting from my mother to Diana. He knows this news will ruin her otherwise perfect wedding day. I swallow hard, feeling vomit threatening to rise in my throat.

Grandpa had a heart attack.

While I was gone.

Logan's voice is a distant echo as he tells my mother the same exact thing he just told me.

"My brother is the county sheriff," he starts, "and he responded to the call."

My grip on Logan's hand tightens and I swallow a lump of vomit.

"The doctor didn't give a detailed report, but he said you should leave as soon as you can in case...in case the treatment doesn't work."

So we can say goodbye.

It's so final.

Harrowing.

My eyes start to flutter shut.

Peter puts his arms around Diana and turns her around, shielding her from the bad news. He might be a slimy bastard, but that look in his eyes tells me all I need to know: he really does love my sister.

My heart is pounding hard against my chest yet at the same time isn't beating at all.

Logan's words resonate in my head but start to lose meaning.

I hear him talking to my parents about plane tickets and being able to get to the airport right away.

He tells me he'll pack my suitcase and will meet me in Indiana as soon as he can.

"What?" I blink, heart in my throat. "You're…you're not coming with me?"

"There are two tickets available on the next flight," he says gently. "You and your mom need to be there. I'll get on the flight after that. It leaves just a few hours later."

I shift my gaze from Logan to my mother, who hasn't spoken to her own father in years. Logan knows Grandpa better than she does. It should be him coming back with me because…because…I need him.

"I can't do this without you."

"Yes," Logan presses. "Yes, you can. Owen will pick you up from the airport. And I'll be there as soon as I can." He grips my hands and starts to move.

"Where are we going?"

"You need to change," he tells me. "And get your carry-on and wallet. I bought your plane tickets."

My lashes come together, and I nod, so grateful for him right now. Plane tickets. Right. I need to get home. To say…to say…I can't finish my thought. Tears fill my eyes, and I reach for the glass of red wine on Diana's table, bringing it to my lips before anyone can stop me.

I get a mouthful down when Logan puts his hand on my wrist, moving the glass away from my mouth.

"Dani," he whispers. "It's going to be okay."

"Is it?" The lump rises in my throat again.

"I don't know. But I hope it will be." He looks down at his phone. "I just texted Quinn."

"Thank you," I tell him, knowing that he texted Quinn to ask Archer to check in on my grandpa. Archer is a general surgeon and won't be caring for Grandpa, but knowing he might be there to talk to me and explain things in terms I'll understand is a little comforting.

"Come on," he urges, brows pushed together. "Let's go upstairs."

~

I SHIFT MY WEIGHT, WATCHING THE SECOND HAND OF THE AIRPORT clock tick by. We have seventeen minutes until we're supposed to line up to board. I'm sitting next to my mother, who's been uncharacteristically quiet this whole time. It's dark out now, and every minute that ticks by kills me.

I won't have cell service in the air.

I won't know what's happening with my grandpa.

Archer called a few minutes ago, going over my grandpa's chart with me and then again with my mom. He could say the same things over and over and I couldn't understand it.

Because I had no idea Grandpa had a history of heart disease. That he'd been seeing a cardiologist for the last five years. Or that it seems like he stopped taking his blood thinners back in the winter.

How didn't I know? Guilt sits heavily in my stomach and made me sick more than once. I hand Mom my purse and hurry to the bathroom once more before we get on the plane. I've gotten rid of all the alcohol in my system this way at least.

"Logan texted you," Mom says, staring straight ahead.

I reach inside my purse and pull out my phone. Logan sent me all the photos he took, saying he hopes it'll offer me a good distraction for a few minutes. I flip through them and wish I could go back to that moment when we were hiking through the Bamboo Forest when everything was fun and new.

Tears fill my eyes, and this time, I make no attempt to quell them. I miss Logan, and I'm terrified of what might happen.

"He's lived a good life," Mom starts, and I jerk my head up, glaring at her.

"Don't," I say as tears roll down my face. "Don't talk like he's already gone. Archer said he's seen people pull through."

"Danielle," Mom whimpers as her own eyes fill with tears. And now I feel bad for her, because of all the time she lost with Grandpa. I've learned more from him in the last year than anyone could have taught me over a lifetime.

We're called to board the plane before she can get another word out, and we silently line up and find our seats. Once we've taken off, Mom reaches into her purse and pulls out a pill bottle filled with Xanax. The strongest sedative I've ever taken is Benadryl, which isn't a sedative at all.

I have an eight-hour flight ahead of me. Against my better judgment, I take one and put it in my mouth. The little white pill crunches between my teeth, leaving a bad taste in my mouth.

I grind it up and let it absorb under my tongue before swallowing hard. I'm sitting next to the window, and turn my head, looking out into the dark. Only a few minutes later, I pass out thanks to the Xanax.

I sleep for a solid five and a half hours. Waking because I have to pee, I carefully step over my mother, who's asleep, as well as the person in the aisle seat. My hair is still done up in a fancy updo, and enough hairspray has been applied to keep things more or less in place. My mascara ran down under my eyes, and I wipe it up, smearing the remaining eyeliner across my cheeks.

I clean myself up the best I can and then go back to my seat, pulling Logan's sweatshirt out of my carry-on bag. He packed it for me, as I sat on the edge of the hotel bed in stunned shock.

I pull it over my head, breathing in deep. I don't know how I would have gotten through this so far without him. He packed my bag, bought my plane ticket, and arranged for the car to come pick us up and take us to the airport.

Dad stayed at the reception, trying to keep Diana from

freaking out. I don't know the appropriate reaction she should have. It's her wedding, after all, and freaking out won't save grandpa. She's never been close to him, not like I have, and there were only two seats left on this plane ride back. Logan will arrive a few hours after I do, and I have no idea if Diana will be with him.

I pull Logan's iPad out of the bag. He downloaded a few things for me to watch, and my heart lurches in my chest when I think about him.

How much I miss him.

How much I need him right now.

And how much I love him.

CHAPTER 25

DANIELLE

"Mom." I gently nudge her. "We're landing."

She sits up, blinking rapidly, and looks around. Maybe she took more Xanax when I wasn't looking, because she slept nearly that entire flight. I don't know the last time I slept for a solid eight hours, and I know that's entirely my fault. I stay up too late doing non-important things, like binging TV shows or finishing a book.

My phone is in my hands, waiting to get the all clear to turn it off airplane mode. It's early in the morning here in Chicago, and I'm terrified for the news I'll get once I get service again. I pack up my bag and look out the window, feeling an odd sense of relief to see Lake Michigan and the flat, green Midwest land below us.

Using my feet, I push the bag under the seat in front of me and grip the armrests. Landing always makes me a little nervous, and I don't have Logan's hand to hold this time.

I turn my phone back on the second we're on the ground and check for updates. A text comes through, but it's from Owen, saying he's almost to the airport to get us. He's here and waiting by the time Mom and I get off the plane. With no bags to get, we hurry through the airport and meet Owen outside.

He pulls me into a hug. "I'm so sorry, Danielle."

"Thank you. And thanks for coming to get us." I sniffle and straighten up, turning to Mom. She's looking at Owen with her mouth hanging open. Right. She has no idea Logan has an identical twin.

"Mom, this is Owen. Logan's twin, obviously. Owen, this is my mom."

"Nice to meet you," he says. "I wish it were under different circumstances."

Mom, who's still a little drugged up, shakes her head. "Yes. I wish so too."

Owen takes our bags and puts them into the trunk of Logan's car, which I'm sure he's driving because it gets much better gas mileage than his truck.

"How's Dexter?" I ask as I get into the passenger seat.

"Driving me crazy. I'll be happy when Logan's back."

"Who's Dexter?" my mom asks.

"Logan's dog," I tell her. "He's a puppy. A giant puppy, but still a puppy."

Owen glances down at my hand, looking for the ring on my finger before pulling out of the parking spot. I'm not sure if he knows what happened between Logan and me yet. Logan isn't one to kiss and tell, but I know it's basically impossible for him to hide anything from Owen. I'll never understand the "twin thing," but it seems basically like mind reading.

"Have you heard from Logan at all?" I ask.

"Yeah, he texted me right before he boarded. His plane left on time. He'll land in a few hours."

A few hours isn't that long. But it seems like an eternity.

"THANK YOU AGAIN," I TELL OWEN AS HE WALKS INTO THE hospital with us.

"You don't have to thank me."

"I know. But…thank you."

"Yes, thank you," Mom echoes.

Owen gives me another hug. "Want me to go up with you?"

I shake my head, heart racing. I'm so nervous my hands shake. I got a call from the hospital not long ago, telling me that Grandpa's condition hasn't changed, which is both good and bad.

He's not getting better.

But he hasn't gotten worse, either.

"No, it's okay. Go home and get some sleep. Are you picking Logan up too?"

Owen shakes his head. "Our dad is. I'll call later and check in, okay? And if you need anything, don't hesitate to call me, Danielle."

"I won't."

"I'm sure my mom will call you later too. We're all here for you."

"Thank you." My eyes fill with tears. Owen's jaw is tense as he says goodbye, turning around and going back to the car. I know what room Grandpa is in, but I'm not familiar with the hospital at all. I ask the attendant at the front desk, and she directs us to an elevator.

"I didn't realize how close you were with Logan's family," Mom says as the elevator doors close. Her voice is void of emotion, and I can't tell if she's simply making a statement or trying to take a jab at me.

"The Dawsons are good people," I tell her. "All of them."

"Logan comes from a big family?"

I nod. "He has two more brothers and a younger sister."

"And one is the sheriff?"

"Yeah. Weston. He's the oldest."

"And you're able to tell Logan apart from his twin?" She

fiddles with the last button on her sweater. Mom is just as scared as I am, and asking me questions is a good distraction.

"I can. I've always been able to, actually. They have completely different personalities, and Owen has a scar on his forehead that's hard to see, but once it's pointed out, it's obvious."

Mom slowly nods her head up and down. "Five children. That's a lot."

"Yeah. It is. But they get along great and going over to Logan's parents' house with everyone is fun."

The elevator stops at the third floor. This hospital is small, old, and more than ready to be knocked down when the new hospital is done. Mom and I hurry to the nurses' station, and we're led to my grandpa's room. He's in the ICU and is hooked up to a bunch of machines. The nurse says he's asleep, but his vitals are holding steady.

Steady, but not improving.

I start crying as soon as I see him, lying there on the bed with his eyes closed. Grandpa naps on the couch at home quite often, and the way he's sleeping now doesn't look like how he sleeps at home.

There's not much color in his cheeks. His arms are straight out at his sides, looking like he was posed and not lying naturally. I can hardly see his chest rising and falling as he breathes. Surviving a heart attack is exhausting, I know, and I just want him to wake up and tell me everything is going to be okay.

"Grandpa," I whisper, and go to him. I sink onto the chair next to the bed and let my head fall down as I cry. "I'm so sorry I wasn't there with you." I curl my fingers around his hand, careful not to bump into the IV line. I sniffle, trying to control my sobs so I don't wake him up. "You wouldn't believe the weekend I had even if I told you."

I swallow hard and pick my head up, wiping my eyes. Mom is still standing in the doorway, tears in her eyes as she looks at her father. I can't even begin to imagine what she's going through right now, and I don't want to.

She's the one who left.

Who turned her back on this town. On her family and friends.

On me.

Grandpa and I tried to get Mom, Dad, and Diana to come for Thanksgiving. And then Christmas.

Grandma's birthday.

The guilt hits me. I spent so many years running from town to town. Hell, I even left the country for a few months. I should have come here from the start. Tears well in my eyes, and I turn my head, unable to keep from crying.

A nurse comes in to check on Grandpa, and Mom talks to her, somehow able to keep it together. I bend my legs up under myself, shivering.

"It's going to be okay," I tell Grandpa and put my hand on his again. "You'll get through this, get back on your medication, and we can go back home. I'll get you one of those 'old person' pill cases too. You know, the ones with the days of the week on them, and I will check it every day and make sure you've taken your pills."

Exhaustion is starting to hit me.

"So," I whisper so quietly I don't think he'd be able to hear me even if he were awake. His hearing has been going, and I have to speak rather loud on a good day. "Logan and I pretended to be engaged." I look at Mom again, who's still talking to the nurse. "And I hiked through the Bamboo Forest and saw three waterfalls. I jumped off a rope swing too." I hold up my arm. "I got a battle wound from it. It's just a surface scratch, but it was enough to freak Di out a bit at first. She was worried how I'd look in pictures. I think it makes me look tough. I'll say I got it from fighting off some sort of wild creature."

My eyes flutter closed, imagining Grandpa laughing at me as he asks if there are any dangerous wild animals in Hawaii. I actually have no idea, but I want to say no since so many tourists walk through that forest and you never hear of anyone getting mauled by bears.

The nurse leaves, and Mom stands at the foot of the bed. I get up, wiping my eyes. "What did she say?" I ask.

Mom opens her mouth to speak but stops, needing a moment to gather her composure. "He has a significant buildup of plaque in his heart. They put a stent in to open up the worst part."

"I know. Archer told us."

Mom's lips press together, and I know the nurse gave her more news…and it's not good. My stomach drops. "He's going to need heart surgery, but right now he's not a good candidate for it."

"What does that mean? If he needs surgery to fix his heart, then he's going to have it."

"Danielle," Mom says gently, and her eyes fill with tears. "The doctor doesn't think his body will be able to handle surgery right now. Grandpa is in pretty bad health and he kept it from us."

"So, they're just going to let him die?" Tears blur my vision, and I angrily shake my head. "I won't allow it. Where's the doctor? I need to talk to him!"

"Honey."

"Don't honey me!" I spit, feeling anxiety wrap around me like a million tiny hands. They're cold, dark, and trying hard to pull me under. "I'm not going to sit here and do nothing if there's a cure for this!"

"There's no cure for heart disease. The stent took care of the worst part, and medication can help control and even reduce the other buildup."

"Why didn't he tell me he was sick? I could have made sure he took his medication and kept up with doctor appointments."

Tears roll down Mom's cheeks. "You know your grandpa."

I sink back into the chair and start silently crying again. Mom comes over and wraps her arm around me. I inhale but don't get any air. My chest heaves, and I want nothing more than for Grandpa to sit up and give me some sort of profound advice that will help me accept this.

"It's not fair, I know," she whispers.

"Why didn't he tell me he was sick?" I take in a shaky breath. "I don't understand."

"I'm sure he didn't want to worry you. The nurse said he'd been dealing with this for years."

"But he seemed fine." I shake my head, feeling so angry at myself for not noticing. He's been slowing down a bit lately, but the man is in his late eighties. I assumed it was normal. "And he… he…" I can't finish my sentence. I start crying again.

I came to Eastwood because I had nowhere else to go. It was a time in my life when I felt like everyone in my life had turned against me. When they were more wrapped up in what the neighbors thought about them than what really mattered.

When I felt like my life was one big failure after another.

And he told me I was lucky to have the opportunity to fail.

Because I was alive.

And being alive isn't anything I should ever take for granted.

I didn't really get it then. But I do now, and the realization makes my heart ache so much it breaks.

Life is so short.

Life is so fleeting.

It's scary to fail. It *hurts* to fail. It's terrifying to not know if you're going to have enough money to live comfortably or just barely cover bills. It sucks to feel all those shitty emotions, the ones that threaten to break you apart and beat you until there's nothing left.

But you can only feel those things if you're alive. And if you're alive, you can change it. Not overnight. Maybe not in a week's time. Or a month. But if you keep living, you can change your life.

And that's what Grandpa wanted me to understand.

I turn back to him and put my hand over his. "I get it," I whisper. "I finally get it now."

Grandpa's fingers twitch and his eyes flutter. Mom and I both gasp, holding our breath as we watch.

"Grandpa?"

"Hey...kiddo." His eyes open and close. Mom goes to get the nurse, and I crouch down next to the bed. The nurse comes in to assess Grandpa, and I stand back, heart in my throat.

He's awake and talked to me. I knew he'd be okay. He'd pull through this.

I grab another tissue and mop up my face, sitting back down in the chair after the nurse leaves. Mom pulls another chair around, sitting on the other side of the bed.

"Carol," Grandpa says, and Mom breaks down.

"You scared us, Dad," Mom cries. "Don't do that again."

Grandpa laughs and then winces. "I don't plan to."

"Why didn't you tell me you were sick?" I ask.

Grandpa slowly shakes his head, widening his eyes. "If I knew I was going to get drilled by you two, I would have told them not to put the stent in."

"That's not funny, Dad." Mom looks up, blinking away tears. "You're not out of the woods yet."

Her words cause the anxiety to rise in my stomach again. It's true, but I don't want to think about that right now. Because the stent is working, and Grandpa is awake and talking to us.

"I know," Grandpa agrees. "You two didn't leave Hawaii for me, did you?"

"We did."

Grandpa shakes his head. "You shouldn't have done that."

Things start to feel better again...and then the doctor comes in, repeating what the nurse said. Grandpa's heart is full of plaque. He's on an aggressive medication regimen now, and it's important to make sure he takes his pills religiously. Grandpa pesters the doctor about going home, grumbling that the only reason he wants him to stay is to collect the insurance money. He'll be here for at least another day.

"See? I'm fine," Grandpa tells us once the doctor leaves.

"You're not, Dad," Mom presses. "And you have to take this seriously."

"Please," I add. "Take it seriously."

Grandpa lets out a breath. "All right. I'll cut back on the greasy food and will take my medication."

"Thank you." I put my hand on Grandpa's again. The nurse comes back in to help sit Grandpa up. They want him up and walking later this morning. I get up, needing to walk around as well. My legs are stiff and my shoulders ache. After a long plane ride, the drive from Chicago to Eastwood, and then sitting tense in that uncomfortable chair, my body is feeling it.

I have three missed calls from Rebecca, and I find a quiet corner to call her back, filling her in on Grandpa's condition. Like Owen, she tells me to call if she needs anything and says she'll be up later once the kids are at her in-laws' house. My phone is dying, and I plug it in when I go back to the room.

A new nurse comes on, and Mom and I both go into the waiting room while she does a full assessment on Grandpa.

"We should get something to eat," Mom tells me as she takes a seat in the waiting room.

"I'm not hungry."

"I'm not either, but it's been a while since either of us ate anything. The food in the cafeteria is bad, I'm sure, but it's better than nothing."

"I guess I could try to eat."

Mom unzips her purse and pulls out a makeup bag. "Dad called while you were out of the room. He said Logan told him something interesting."

"Interesting?" I look at my mom, watching her fix her eyeliner. Did Logan tell Dad the engagement is a hoax? If he did...I don't care. It doesn't matter compared to what's going on right now.

"Logan told him that you said you don't want to go back to grad school."

"I...I don't."

Mom almost drops her mirror. "You're kidding, right?"

My mouth opens, and I slowly shake my head. "You're really doing this now?"

"We want what's best for you. Grandpa would agree."

All the frustration I've been feeling over the years threatens to bubble up and explode. My heart is ripping in two, all while my stomach churns. I don't know if I'm going to throw up, scream, or start throwing things.

"No," I say, voice small. "No, he wouldn't." I stare at my mother in disbelief, wishing I could write this off as her trying to distract herself from what's actually going on. But I know better, and once Dad gets here, I'm sure he'll get on me about it too.

"I understood why you came here," Mom goes on. That's bullshit too. She's so wrapped up in trying to impress people, in making friends only so she can drop their names to others, in constantly having to one-up each other. She doesn't get it, and I don't think she ever will.

But I'm done with that. Done with not knowing who was with me or against me or who was using me or talking behind my back. Done with hanging around people who wrote the definition of *first world problems* and care more with the pH levels in their pools than the pollution in our oceans.

"But now it's time to leave."

"I don't want to leave." I close my eyes and tears roll down my cheeks. "I like it here. It's not fancy, and we don't have five-star restaurants or Ivy League colleges nearby, but this is home. The people in this town are great, and I like my job."

"You're a bartender," Mom spits. "You are better than that."

"I'm not better than anyone." I shake my head. "And under

normal circumstances, your job doesn't define you. I mean, if I were a drug dealer, I'd say my line of work spoke volumes about my character, but I go to work and work hard. What's the difference between me tending bars and working in an office?"

"Your paycheck. It's a big difference."

"I don't need to be rich to be happy."

"Stop being ridiculous," Mom goes on. "Money might not buy happiness, but it sure as hell makes your life easier. You'll always have bills to pay and not having to worry if you'll have enough can take so much stress off you."

"But I can pay my bills. I don't have much, but I really am happy. Why is that so hard to believe?"

Mom slowly shakes her head. "I don't want to watch you throw your life away."

I clench my fists. "Then don't."

CHAPTER 26

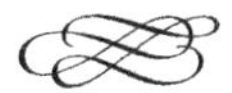

LOGAN

Danielle is sitting in the waiting room. Her legs are curled up under her and her head is resting against the wall. She's wearing black leggings and my sweatshirt, and my heart swells in my chest when I see her through the glass doors. I have to get buzzed into the ICU waiting area, and Danielle gets up as soon as she sees me.

I take her in my arms, hugging her tight and holding her close.

"How is he?"

"Um," she starts, letting out a shaky breath. "Stable for now. He was in really bad shape, and he's so lucky the paramedics got him here in time."

"That sounds promising."

She nods. "I thought so too, but the doctor isn't as optimistic."

"And how are you?"

"I'm…shaken but okay. And I'm still just shocked to hear that he was so sick. I had no idea. I mean…I saw some changes but wrote it off as him aging. You slow down when you get old."

"He was acting just fine before we left."

"I know, and that's what scares me." Danielle rubs her forehead. "The doctor said he's at risk for another heart attack or even a stroke. His blood pressure was out of control and still needs to be closely monitored. He's leaving in just two days." She shakes her head. "It seems soon, doesn't it?"

"Yeah, but it'll be good for him to get out of here. He'll be able to move around, which is important."

She nods, and her eyes fill with tears.

"I'm sorry," she squeaks out, voice tight.

"Hey, it's okay." I take her in my arms again, cradling her against my chest. We sit on a bench, and Danielle wraps her arms around me as she cries. I rub her back, wishing I could make her better.

"I hope so." I reach over and grab a tissue for her. She wipes her eyes and blows her nose. "I must look so gross."

"No. You look like someone who's been through a lot in the last few hours. Do you need anything? Coffee? Food?"

"I'm thirsty."

"I'll get you something."

"I'll come with you."

We get up and go to the vending machine in the hall outside the waiting area. Danielle has to be so exhausted, and I'm sure she's going to stay here for the rest of the day. She gets a water and we go back into the waiting room. Danielle rests her head against my shoulder, and I put my arm around her.

She puts the water bottle down and hooks one arm around my waist, getting as comfortable as she can on this couch. I run my fingers through her hair. She's right about to fall asleep when there's a commotion inside the ICU. Danielle jerks up and then gasps when she sees the nurses rushing into a room.

"That's my grandpa's room."

Holding her hand in mine, we go through another set of doors and to her grandpa's room. Her mother is standing in the corner, out of the way of the nurses who are working on her grandpa.

"What's happening?" Danielle's eyes fill with tears, and her mother comes over.

"We were talking, and he just…he just…stopped breathing."

"No." Danielle shakes her head back and forth. "No, no, no!"

She turns to me, tears streaming down her face. The nurses start doing CPR, and we stand there, watching in horror as the heart monitor starts to flatline. I wrap Danielle in my arms, turning her away. She doesn't need to see this. She doesn't need this to be the last memory she has of her grandpa.

~

"DANIELLE?" I SAY SOFTLY, TURNING THE CAR OFF. WE JUST PULLED into the driveway of the farmhouse. We left the hospital, and Danielle said she wanted to go home. Her mother is in the back-seat, and no one said a word on the drive here.

But what do you say after something like this?

Carol and I get out, and she heads up to the house. Danielle hasn't moved. I open the door and reach in, unbuckling her seatbelt.

"Do you want to go to my house instead?" I ask, knowing it's going to be hard for her to step foot inside the house.

She blinks, and fat tears roll down her face. "No. I…I…I'm sorry."

"Don't be sorry." I extend my hand. "Take your time."

Nodding, she wipes her eyes and takes my hand. We walk up the front porch steps together. Her mom already went inside. Danielle hesitates before she crosses the threshold. More tears spill from her eyes, and I hate seeing her hurt like this.

If I could take it all away, I would.

"I want to lie down," she tells me.

"Want me to come with you?"

She nods, and we go upstairs and get into her bed. Danielle pulls the blankets up over her and turns to me, burying her head against my chest as she cries. I rub her back until she falls asleep. Carefully moving out of bed so I don't wake her up, I tuck her in and go downstairs.

Carol is in the kitchen, with a bottle of Jack on the counter.

"My father and I didn't see eye to eye on most things," she starts, pouring a small amount of whiskey in a glass. "But we both cared about the girls." She drinks the whiskey. "I'm glad Danielle has you."

"Yeah. She does have me."

Carol adds another splash of whiskey to the glass. "I…I need to make funeral arrangements. Will you stay with Danielle?"

"Of course. Do you need anything?" I run my hand through my hair, not sure what I can do to help.

Carol blinks away tears. "No, thank you though." One of the cats jumps up on the counter, and Carol shoos it away. "Actually, do you know where the cat food is? I think they are hungry?"

I go into the pantry but don't find any food. "Looks like you're all out. I can run out and get some."

"That would be helpful. Thank you." Carol looks at the cat that's twisting around her ankles. "I don't know their names."

"They're easy. There's Black Cat, Orange Cat, and Tabby Cat."

She smiles and blinks back tears. "That sounds like my dad."

"And the horses are Sundance, Bailey, and Alibi."

"Oh my God. I forgot about them. I don't know anything about horses."

"We had horses when we were kids. My sister was into showing for a while. I'll take care of them too." And the chickens and goats, but I don't bring them up. Carol seems overwhelmed enough as it is.

"Thank you," she says again, and this time has a harder time controlling her emotions. I go outside to check on the horses first. Luckily, they were out in the pasture and not in their stalls, and have access to grass, water, and shade. I top off their water trough and give each horse a scoop of grain before heading out to the store.

Quinn calls as I turn onto the road.

"How's Danielle?" she asks.

"Really sad. She just fell asleep, and I'm leaving to get cat food for her grandpa's cats."

"That's all you need?"

"Yeah. They're out."

"Come here. I'm only a few miles away and have more than enough. I can give you enough to last a few days."

"Thanks. That saves me a trip into town."

"I'll see you in a bit then. The front door is unlocked. I just put Emma down for a nap so come on in."

I end the call and drive to Quinn's, going in through the front door and silently closing it behind me. I find Quinn in the kitchen.

"Are you making a bomb?" I ask, looking at the computer parts and wires on the table.

Quinn arches an eyebrow. "Yes, Logan. I'm making a bomb." She shakes her head. She flips something over. "I'm making a robot."

"For fun?"

"Yeah. Why else do you build robots?"

"You are such a nerd."

She narrows her eyes. "You won't be calling me a nerd when this bad boy wins the robot fight."

"Just hearing you say *robot fight* makes you an even bigger nerd."

She puts down a pair of pliers and gets up, going into her pantry to get the cat food. "I feel so bad for Danielle."

"Me too. It was the last thing we expected. One minute we're dancing and drinking at the reception, and the next, Weston is calling."

"How was the wedding and pretending you two were

engaged?" Quinn puts several cans of cat food into a cloth grocery bag and hands it to me.

"It was fun, actually. And everyone bought our fake engagement."

"Really?"

"You sound surprised."

Quinn wrinkles her nose and picks up one of her million cats, bringing it out of the pantry so she can close the door. "I am. I didn't think you'd be able to pull it off. I mean…didn't people wonder when you weren't being all affectionate?" She puts her hand on her stomach and makes a face.

"You okay, sis?"

"Don't change the subject."

"You look like you're going to puke."

She holds up her hand. "There's a good chance I might."

"Are you pregnant again?"

She pulls her lips over her teeth and nods. "I just found out yesterday. Only Archer knows. We were going to tell everyone tonight, but we'll wait a few days until after the funeral and everything."

"You're serious?"

"Yeah. Emma is going to be a big sister."

I smile and give Quinn a one-armed hug. "Congrats!"

"Thanks. I feel like this is the worst timing to tell you, but you did ask. Anyway…tell me about Hawaii." She goes to the fridge and gets out a sparkling water. "How did you convince everyone you were really engaged?"

"It wasn't hard."

Quinn raises an eyebrow. "Really? You're not the best actor."

"I didn't have to act."

Quinn narrows her eyes, studying me. Out of all my siblings, Quinn and I are the most alike. Other than the year when I referred to her only as "Nadine the Butt Doctor" when we were kids, we've—for the most part—gotten along.

"Did Danielle?"

"At first, but then…"

"Oh my God! You guys finally hooked up?"

"Finally?"

Quinn gives me a look. "Everyone knows you've been crushing on Danielle since the day you met her. Does Scarlet know? We were so hoping this would happen!"

I shake my head. "You both need a hobby."

"It'll be Owen next since you and Danielle are finally together."

"That's charity, not a hobby. And Danielle and I…I don't know."

"Wait. You hooked up but aren't together?" Quinn sits at the large island counter.

"We never had a chance to talk about it. We didn't leave much time for talking."

"Gross."

"I don't want her to think what happened was just a hookup," I say, feeling really fucking grateful for my sister right now. It used to be me giving her relationship advice and not the other way around. But Quinn is smart, and now she's married with a kid and another on the way. If I were to take anyone's advice, it would be hers.

"You love her, don't you?" she says gently.

"Yeah. I do."

"Then tell her."

CHAPTER 27

DANIELLE

I open my eyes and roll over. I don't know what time it is. Or what day it is. All I know is Logan is in bed next to me, and his slow and steady breathing is the only thing keeping me from falling apart. Everything happened so fast.

We got to the hospital. Grandpa seemed like he was going to pull through. And then he was gone.

I slowly get out of bed, needing to use the bathroom. Logan hasn't even gone home yet since he got back to Eastwood. Everything was so perfect before, and I would give anything to go back to our last night in Hawaii.

After using the bathroom, I go downstairs, following the sound of the TV. Mom is in the living room, drinking wine and watching a baking show. It's almost four in the morning.

"Mom?"

"Oh, Danielle, honey. You're up."

"So are you. Did you get any sleep?"

"A bit here and there."

I cross my arms over my chest, chilled even though it's warm in the house. Usually, we'd turn the air conditioning up before going to bed. I hate waking up all sweaty.

But at least I get to wake up.

"Want some company?"

"Yeah, that would be nice." Mom sets her glass of wine down and pats the couch next to her. Orange Cat is curled up on her lap. "Dad is on a plane right now, and Diana and Peter will be here on Tuesday for the memorial service. You know it was your grandpa's wish not to have a traditional funeral, right?"

I nod. "Yeah, he mentioned it a few times. Said they were a waste of money and he just wants his ashes scattered in the field where Grandma's are."

"It's fitting." Mom's eyes get watery. Both her parents are gone now, and that has to feel so sad and so strange.

I sit on the couch next to Mom. "I made a bunch of Grandma's pies a few weeks ago."

"How'd they turn out?"

"Logan liked them. The apple was better than the peach, but I used canned peaches instead of fresh like the recipe said to."

"Grandma always used fresh everything. She was one of the healthiest eaters I knew, and that was back before clean eating was a fad."

I smile, looking from the TV to the framed photos of Grandma and Grandpa on the wall. "I wish I could have met her."

"She would have loved you. And been so proud, just like Grandpa was. And he was so, so proud of you, Danielle."

My throat gets all tight as I try not to cry. "I'm really going to miss him."

"I know." Mom puts her arm around me. "I know. But it'll get easier."

I nod because that's what I'm supposed to do. Tell myself that it gets easier. Remind myself that Grandpa lived a long, good life.

Say it was his time. That he's with God now. Reunited with Grandma.

But it doesn't make it any easier.

~

"HEY." LOGAN STEPS INTO THE KITCHEN, LOOKING AT THE MESS ALL over the counter. "I woke up and you weren't in bed anymore."

"I couldn't sleep." I look out into the living room at Mom, who fell asleep on the couch. It's going on nine-thirty AM now. "And I couldn't sit still."

Logan comes over to the counter, sliding one hand over my back. "My mom bakes when she's upset too. She says it keeps her busy, and cupcakes make everyone happy."

I smile, wiping flour off my hands. "I'm nowhere near as good at decorating cakes as your mom is."

"I don't care how they look as long as they taste good."

"Agreed."

Logan pushes my hair out of my face. "How are you doing?"

"I think…I think I'm okay."

"It's okay not to be okay right now," he says gently.

"I know." My eyes fill with tears again, and I wrap my arms around Logan. My chest tightens and a strangled sob escaped my lips. He holds me tight, standing there for as long as I need him to. When I'm able to breathe normally again, I straighten up and look into Logan's eyes. "I'm tired," I confess.

"Go upstairs and lie down. I'll clean up."

"I don't want to make you—"

"You're not. I'm offering."

My throat feels tight again and I nod, knowing if I open my mouth to talk there's a good chance I'm going to start crying. I go upstairs and get back into bed. Usually, I lie awake thinking about everything that upsets me, worries me, or makes me anxious.

But right now, I feel nothing.

And I don't know if the numbness is worse or better than the bad feelings.

Eventually, I fall asleep. Mom wakes me up a few hours later, saying Dad is here and brought pizza. Logan stays and eats with us, and then goes back to his place to change and shower. I miss him as soon as he's gone.

Everything happened so fast with Grandpa...and also with Logan.

We went to Hawaii as friends. And we left as...I don't know. We're not just friends anymore. I feel more for him than I've ever felt for anyone. I'm not in the mental space to start worrying about changing my relationship status on social media, and I don't think Logan and I need a label like that anyway.

Because he's still my best friend...who's now my boyfriend.

I think.

We slept together multiple times and holy hell, it was good. I want to do it again...just when I'm not so sad.

After showering and changing into sleeper shorts and an oversized t-shirt, I go downstairs and find my parents at the dining room table. Dad is going over Grandpa's finances. The farm has been paid off for years, and while Grandpa didn't have much, he had just enough saved up to live off of while still caring for his animals.

"Hey, honey," Mom says, looking up from the papers. Dad closes a folder as soon as I step into the room. "Did you get some rest?"

I shake my head. "I did shower, though. I'm going to go check on the horses. Their stalls need to be cleaned, I'm sure. Guess I'll be taking another shower." I look around the house, knowing it's going to be so weird and so quiet once my parents leave in a few days.

The thought of being here without grandpa makes my heart ache all over again.

"Do you remember Sandra Harris?" Dad asks as he stacks the papers.

"From your work? Yeah."

"She's pregnant and is due any day now. She plans to take twelve weeks off and then come back."

"Why are you telling me this?" A weird hollow feeling starts to rise inside me. I know exactly why Dad is telling me this, and that's not what's causing the feeling. What's causing the feeling is that in the back of my mind, running away from the farm seems like it would be easy.

I wouldn't have to be alone in this house, being reminded over and over that Grandpa is gone. People wouldn't look at me with pity and give me sad smiles while asking how I'm holding up.

It's my thing to do when the going gets tough. Run away as fast as I can, giving myself a head start before my problems catch up with me.

But the thing is...they always do.

And this time...this time leaving would hurt even more than staying.

CHAPTER 28

LOGAN

"How's Danielle doing?" Owen asks, moving an empty casserole dish from the counter to the sink. We're at her house, and the service for her grandpa just ended. A few people are still at the house, sharing stories and memories. Her grandpa was respected by the town, and we are all feeling his loss. I think half the town turned up today, bringing flowers and food and giving their condolences. That's the thing with small towns. When you know most everyone, you care for most everyone.

"She's trying to keep it together." I open the fridge, trying to find a place to put the bowl of taco salad someone brought. It won't fit, and I'm pretty sure the extra fridge in the basement is full already too.

The last few days passed in a blur. Danielle cried, slept, and drank a lot, and then when the rest of her family came into town, the time was spent reflecting on her grandpa's life and looking through scrapbooks. Now everything is over, and people are leaving.

Stacking the bowl of taco salad on top of another casserole, I go down into the basement to try and make things fit. It takes a bit of rearranging, but I get the two dishes put in. Danielle is on the back porch, and I'm about to go out with her when I see her father sitting on a chair next to her.

The windows are open, letting in the warm breeze.

"Have you thought more about my offer?" I hear her father say, making me pause. "We could really use someone with your business savvy."

"I…I don't know," Danielle tells him, and my heart falls to the floor. "It would just be temporary?"

"Yes, unless you decide to stay. There is a chance Sandra won't want to come back. She says she plans on it now, but I wouldn't be surprised if she stayed home for the next year."

Danielle lets out a breath and wipes her eyes. "I don't know," she repeats. "The house is going to feel so empty after everyone leaves."

I tear myself away, not wanting to eavesdrop anymore. If leaving is what Danielle needs to do…fuck. I don't know.

"You okay?" Owen asks when I come back onto the kitchen. "I mean, besides the obvious. You seem…you seem different."

"I'm tired," I tell him, which is true. I've never been able to lie to Owen. It feels wrong, and he's just able to sense the truth, much like I can with him.

"Take Danielle upstairs, rock her world again, and then pass out."

"I don't think she's in the mood for that."

Owen knows we got together but hasn't pressed me to take things further because of everything else that happened. It's not the right time to sit down and talk about relationships. Danielle is dealing with enough. I've waited for her this long, giving her the time she needs.

Wanting her to stay…telling her that it will kill me if she leaves…it feels selfish.

~

"THANKS." DANIELLE TAKES THE CUP OF COFFEE FROM ME AS I SIT on the steps of the front porch next to her. Everyone has left, including her parents and sister. The sun set not long ago, and it's just the two of us here at the house.

She takes a sip of coffee and sets the cup on the porch next to her and rests her head on my shoulder. I slip my arm around her waist, and Danielle twists, pressing her forehead against mine. Tears well in her eyes, spilling down when I kiss her.

Desperation hits us both at the same time, and the moment our lips connect, Danielle moves closer, straddling me right here on the porch. She's wearing a black dress, and I pull it up to her waist. Spreading her legs, she rocks her hips over mine and then brings her hands down to undo my pants. She scrambles to remove my pants, and I slip my hand under her dress, pulling her panties down. I stroke her clit before she climbs back on, guiding my cock to her core.

She slowly lowers herself onto me, wrapping her arms around my shoulders. I put my lips to her neck, kissing and sucking at her skin as she rocks herself up and down. Pressing herself down, she arches her back, digging her fingers into my flesh. A car drives down the road, and we both freeze.

The house is set back and it's dark out. But the porch lights are on, and the front yard is flat and mowed.

"Should we go inside?" Danielle asks, moving her pelvis in a slow circle that feels so fucking amazing.

"Yeah," I grunt, not wanting to stop. Danielle and I break apart and stand, but only make it a few steps before we fall back together again. I grab her around the waist and spin her around so her ass is pressed against my cock. She grips the porch railing, bending over so I can enter her.

Reaching around, I work her clit as I thrust in and out of her tight pussy. She tosses her head back, moaning as she comes. The second her pussy contracts around my cock, I come as well, moving my hand from between her legs to her stomach.

It's the first time we've had sex since Hawaii, and while everything came on fast, borne out of desperation of needing to be close, it didn't disappoint. There will never be another woman in this world who turns me on as much as Danielle.

I kiss her neck and pull out, shuffling back and trying not to trip over my pants which are around my ankles.

"Next time we'll go on the back porch," I say as Danielle spins around in my arms.

"I like the sound of that plan."

I kiss her forehead, and we go inside with the intention of showering together, but then Danielle remembers she has to bring the horses in from the pasture and feed all the other animals.

She changes into leggings and a t-shirt, and I go out with her.

"I took care of the horses a lot," she says, sliding the big barn door open. "I like them. But it suddenly feels like Grandpa did everything."

I put my arm around her shoulders, kissing the top of her head as we walk. "He did a lot."

"It's overwhelming," she admits. "I don't know how I'm going to take care of everything on my own."

"You won't have to on your own. I'll help. Hell, we can even get Owen over here cleaning stalls."

Danielle smiles up at me, eyes watery again. "Thanks. I'll figure out a routine eventually. Though I guess this means I'm going to have to start getting up early. I am not a morning person."

"I know. I don't think anyone really is. Those who say they are, are lying. Just like people who say they like running."

"You like working out." She gives me a pointed look.

"That's different. And I do."

We get the animals taken care of and go inside, showering this time. Danielle grabs a bottle of cheap red wine that someone brought over, along with a tray of cookies. We sit on the couch and find something funny to watch. Danielle pours two big glasses of wine and settles in my arms, saying she just wants to watch TV and not think about anything for a while.

By the time the movie ends, we're both lying down and half-asleep. I turn the TV off and spoon my body around Danielle's. She hasn't been sleeping well lately, and I know she's tired. I run my fingers through her hair until she falls asleep.

I'm hot under the blanket with her, and there's a lump in the couch that's pressing against my spine. I'm uncomfortable, but I don't even think about moving. Because lying here with Danielle is the only place I want to be.

CHAPTER 29

DANIELLE

I lean against the metal gate, watching the horses run around the pasture. The chickens are already fed, and the goats are grazing near the barn. It's a little after eight in the morning, which is still early for me but not as early as Grandpa got up to feed the animals.

I can handle eight AM. Well, when the weather is nice, that is. I'm already dreading having to trudge out here in the rain and snow.

Logan was still asleep on the couch when I came out here, and I silently go back into the house, not wanting to wake him. He's been my rock the last few days, and I really don't think I could have gotten through this without him.

I'm making breakfast when my phone rings, and I hurry to silence the call. It's a local number, but since I don't know who it is, I don't answer. If it's important, they'll leave a message. And I really don't feel like talking to anyone right now anyway.

Looking around the kitchen, I feel an emptiness in my heart. I want it to go away. I want to be happy again.

I know I will be, but it'll take time.

Logan helps. I smile when I think about him, and look

through the kitchen into the living room at him. All three cats are on the couch with him, and I grab my phone to take a picture so I can tease him about being a crazy cat lady just like Quinn later. The floor creaks as I walk out of the living room, and the cats jump off the couch, meowing and begging for their food.

Logan comes into the kitchen as I'm feeding them.

"Morning." He's rubbing his neck.

I spoon the canned food into three bowls. "Morning. Did you sleep funny or something?"

"Yeah, and it makes me feel old to wake up sore."

"I'll rub your shoulders. We have seven minutes until the pancake casserole is done."

He sits at the island counter. "I didn't know pancake casseroles were a thing."

"I didn't either, but it smells good, doesn't it?"

"Yeah. It does."

I plug in the coffee pot. "I'm on the schedule to work today."

"Don't worry about it. Take the week off if you need it."

"Sleeping with the boss has its perks."

Logan chuckles. "Just one of many, I hope."

"I kind of want to work. The distraction would be nice."

"It's up to you, Danielle. No one expects you to come in yet, and if you decide you need to leave after a while, you can."

I push my hair back and nod, going around Logan. "Thanks. I'll give that a try." I put my hands on his neck and start massaging his muscles. He's only wearing boxers, and having him walk around the house half-naked like this is something I could get used to.

Dad calls as we're eating breakfast, and I go to silence the call but answer it at the last second.

"Sandra went into labor early," Dad says as soon as I pick up.

"Oh, wow. Is the baby okay?"

"I assume so. I didn't ask."

I shake my head, glad he can't see my expression right now. "So you need to fill her spot right away."

"We do. And your mother knows a great real estate agent in Indianapolis and is sure she can get her to get the farm listed and sold in record time."

"What? I…I…" Sell the farm? Hell no. This place was Grandma and Grandpa's dream. There is no way I'm letting them sell this place…but I don't see how I have much of a choice. With Grandpa gone, Mom would inherit everything.

It's hers to sell, and I know she'll be happy to have this place off her hands. She thinks I'm marrying Logan, so not having a house shouldn't be a big deal to me. But it is.

Because this is the only home I have.

The same number that called earlier calls me again.

"I'm getting another call," I tell Dad. "I'll call you back later, okay?" I end the call and send the other caller to voicemail again.

"What baby?" Logan asks.

I trade my phone for my fork. "Someone that works for my dad had her baby early. So now there's an open position at the company until she comes back from maternity leave."

"And your dad wants you to fill in."

"Yeah. He told me about it yesterday, and tried to spin it as a temporary thing, saying it would be good experience and could help me take the bar's business to the next level."

"Oh, right. They think we're getting married."

I nod. "I'm sure he's thinking if he can get us to do long distance for a few weeks, it'll show me I can do grad school too."

"What do you want to do?"

My dad texts me before I can answer Logan. "He said he'll pay me her salary, and wow, she made good money."

Logan looks up from his food, and maybe it's silly, but I desperately want him to tell me he doesn't want me to even think about going away.

Because he loves me.

Just like I love him.

But he doesn't, making me think that maybe I was wrong about this all along.

I SIT ON THE BACK PORCH, LOOKING OUT AT THE PASTURE. LOGAN left after breakfast, needing to go home, take care of Dexter, and get ready for work. My heart is getting heavy again, and while I never really talked about my love life with Grandpa—mostly because I didn't have one—I wish I could get his advice right now.

Logan and I have been really good friends for a year now. And we took things to the next level only recently, but telling him I love him, and wanting to hear him tell it to me, seems fitting.

But is it too soon?

"I have a feeling you'd tell me it doesn't matter," I say to the sky. "That it's never too soon for love or something like that." I close my eyes and let out a breath. "And I know…I can be the one to tell him too. If he doesn't love me, then…then I'll have to deal with it."

I swallow hard, getting scared at just the thought of following my heart. If I follow my head and my head is wrong, I can try again. But if I follow my heart and my heart is wrong, it might break. And I don't think I can survive another broken heart.

Rebecca texts me, asking how I'm doing. I reply and go to set my phone down but then remember I never listened to the voicemail from that unknown number. It's a lawyer, asking me to call him back.

I hate all the legalities that come with death.

As if it's not enough to have to learn to live with your loss, you have to worry about bills and utilities and taxes. I watch the horses graze and start to feel anxiety rise in my stomach again, making my hands shake. I don't make enough to be able to feed them. I've only just started building my savings back up, and if I want to try and keep all the animals, I'm going to have to pick up a lot more shifts at the bar.

Like one every single night and go back to low cut shirts and letting gross men hit on me so I can get bigger tips. I shudder at the thought, not sure if I'm capable of sinking that low.

The secretary at the lawyer's office answers right away and transfers me over.

"Hi, Ms. Cross," the lawyer starts. "First of all, I'm very sorry for your loss."

"Thank you."

"Would you be able to come into the office sometime today? We have some paperwork to take care of."

"Uh, sure. I thought my mother took care of it all."

"She and your father did, but they weren't able to sign everything."

"They weren't?"

"They couldn't. Because your grandfather left his house and property to you."

CHAPTER 30

LOGAN

I sit in the driveway, drumming my fingers on the steering wheel. I just left Danielle's house and got home, but I haven't gone inside yet. My mind is racing, and my heart is beating fast right along with it.

I love her.

I don't want her to leave, even if it's just for a few weeks. But I don't want to be selfish, because she's going through a hard time right now, and if getting away from Eastwood is what she needs, then she should go.

But will she come back?

She came here because her grandpa was here, and now that he's gone…what's going to keep her here?

Me.

Maybe. Maybe not.

"Fuck," I swear under my breath. For the last year I've wanted to tell her that I love her. We finally made love, and it was incredible. She's incredible.

We are incredible together.

I close my eyes and lean my head back against the seat.

And then Owen knocks on the window. "Dude, what the hell are you doing?" he asks, opening the passenger side door.

"Trying to decide if I should tell Danielle I love her, or if it's unfair to drop that on her when she has a good reason to get out of town for a little bit. But if she leaves, will she come back? She doesn't have a reason to."

"You're a fucking idiot, you know that, right?"

I glare at my twin.

"Stop overthinking things like you always do. You love her. Go tell her and be her reason to stay. Now. Or give me your clothes, and I'll go over there and pretend to be you."

"It won't work with Danielle."

Owen's brows go up. "Exactly."

I get what he isn't saying just as much as what he is. Danielle's always been able to tell us apart when most people can't. She says she can sense the difference, and jokes that she's more attracted to the energy I put off over Owen.

"Get out of my car."

Owen claps me on the back. "Go get 'em, tiger."

I start the car, putting it in reverse before Owen is fully out. It takes twelve minutes to drive to Danielle's house from ours, and I get there in less than ten. I put the car in park and forget to take my seatbelt off in my desperation to get to Danielle.

I race up the front porch steps, getting to the last one when she opens the door. When I left, she was still in PJs with her hair in a messy bun. Now she's wearing a rainbow-striped skirt and a white tank top. Her hair is braided, and she's wearing makeup. An oversized bag hangs from her shoulder.

Is she leaving?

"Logan!" she exclaims, not expecting to see me. I grab her around the waist and pull her close, putting my lips to hers. I kiss her hard, feeling my heart flutter in my chest.

"I love you, and I don't want you to leave." The words come out easier than I expected them to.

Danielle straightens up and blinks. "What?" She sets the bag down. "I mean…what?"

I inhale and run my hands down her arms, stepping closer and looking into her eyes. "I've been in love with you pretty much since we met. You were always so adamant about not staying here and not wanting to date so I tried to ignore my feelings for you, but they never went away. I really love being your best friend, but I want to be your boyfriend. And who knows, maybe your real fiancé someday."

Danielle's lips part and tears well in her eyes again. "I love you too."

"You do?"

"Yes," she says, and the tears spill down her face. "I've been in love with you for a long time too but didn't want to admit it to myself. And then when we finally kissed…I knew I was a goner."

"If you need to leave Eastwood, I get it."

She shakes her head. "I'm not leaving Eastwood. My grandpa left the farm and the house to me. I was going to go into town and finish signing the papers. My parents knew, and they didn't say anything." She shakes her head. "I'm so tired of them trying to force my hand. But this is home now. My home. Maybe it could be our home," she adds softly.

"Are you asking me to move in with you? Geez, Dani, I just told you I love you. We should slow down. Wait another year before we take the next step."

"You're still a jerk," she laughs, shaking her head as I go in for another kiss. "You are my best friend." She takes her lips off mine just enough to talk. "You'll always be my best friend."

"And you'll always be mine."

"Tell me you love me again. I like hearing it."

"I love you, Danielle Cross." I cup her face in my hands. "And I know things haven't gone as you thought they would, but I like to believe everything led you to me."

Another tear rolls down her cheek, and I wipe it away with

my thumb. "It did," she whispers. "I was so busy trying to find my place in the world and fit in, I didn't realize that I was right where I was supposed to be all along. With you."

CHAPTER 31

DANIELLE

Logan puts his lips to mine again, and I wrap my arms around his shoulders. I love this man so much. He is the best friend I could ask for, and the best relationships are built on a foundation of respect and friendship. We just fit together, and I know I'll never find another person in the whole world who gets me better than Logan Dawson.

Things feel the same between us, and yet everything has changed.

"Do you need to go to the lawyer now?" he asks between kisses.

"I should."

"Want me to come with you?"

"You'll be bored." His lips go to my neck, and I start to melt against him. "Hell, I'll be bored. But it would be nice to have you with me."

Logan pulls me into a tight embrace, and I rest my head against his chest and listen to his heart beating. My eyes fall shut, and for the first time since we left Hawaii, I don't feel like I'm spiraling out of control.

Things are still messy. Things are still going to hurt for a while. But that's life, isn't it? It's not about going through it and having everything fall perfectly into place. It's about the people you have on the ride with you.

The ones who hold your hand.

Who help you up when you fall.

Who love you.

CHAPTER 32

LOGAN

"I think that's the last of it." I set a box down in the foyer and run my hand over my forehead, wiping away beads of sweat. We picked the hottest day yet this summer to move in together.

Smiling, Danielle looks around the farmhouse. "Now the fun begins, and we get to organize everything."

"That does not sound like fun."

She laughs and grabs my hand, pulling me into the kitchen for something to drink before we go back to figuring out what to do with everything. For now, we've been sleeping in Danielle's bed in the room she's always stayed in. Eventually, we plan on taking over the master bedroom, but Danielle isn't ready for that yet.

It's been pretty much untouched since her grandpa passed only a month ago, and I'm in no rush to have her go through his things before we totally redecorate it. Moving in together only a few weeks after we made things official might seem too soon to some people, but it made sense to us. We've been friends for so long. We know each other.

We love each other, and we don't want to wait any longer.

Dexter runs up the stairs, chasing one of the cats. He's been at it all day and has gotten his nose scratched more than once already. You'd think he'd learn…

Danielle fills two glasses with ice water and grabs a folder from the kitchen table, looking at applications. We're hiring new help at the bar and need to start the interview process this week. And then next week we're expanding our hours again.

"No work," I tell her and close the folder. "It's our day off."

Danielle has been in charge of the expansion and is having way more fun with it than she should.

"Fine. You're all sweaty and need to shower. I should probably go up and help you."

"You should. Make sure I've washed all the hard-to-reach places." I take a big drink of water and then take Danielle in my arms. She pushes me away laughing, telling me I stink and am getting sweat on her. Of course I just hold her tighter. She slips out of my arms and tries to run away.

I dodge around the counter and pick her up and toss her over my shoulder. She laughs and protests, and I carry her into the living room and playfully toss her on the couch and move on top of her.

"Shower, now!" she laughs, grabbing the hem of my shirt and pulling it up over my head. "We have to leave soon to be at your parents on time anyway."

"Right." I kiss her neck and get up, pulling her to her feet. We're having dinner with my family tonight, and I have something important to ask Danielle before we leave. Dexter tears through the house again, and Tabby Cat jumps up onto the couch to try and get away from him. Dex launches himself at the cat, knocking over a lamp in the process.

"They have claws, buddy," I tell him, pulling him off the couch. "I really hope this is just a phase."

"Let's hope so. Dex hasn't been around the cats that much."

Before officially moving in, I started bringing Dexter over to try and ease him into moving, but he's such a doofus most the time nothing seems to faze him. I pet him for a minute before Danielle and I go upstairs to shower.

I pull a small box out of my drawer while she's drying her hair and put it in my back pocket. It's too big and is obvious. Wearing a jacket would be even more obvious since it's hot as hell outside tonight. I wrap my fingers over the box and go downstairs, impatiently watching TV until Danielle is ready to go.

We go into the barn before leaving, checking to make sure the animals have enough water on this hot ass day. Danielle stops next to the pasture gate, taking a few seconds to look around.

"It's so pretty out today."

"And hot."

She makes a face. "I kind of like the heat. Mostly because I don't have to do any sort of physical labor in it and can just lie out and tan."

"I do like looking out and seeing you tan."

She wiggles her eyebrows. "That's because I tan topless."

"It's not bad in the shade," I tell her, motioning to a large oak tree near the barn. Taking her hand, I start toward it, hoping she won't question anything. We have to go this way to get to the car anyway.

"I do like this spot."

We pause under the tree, and I dig the little box out of my pocket, holding it down at my side so Danielle doesn't notice.

"I love you," I tell her.

"I love you, too." She smiles up at me. "So much." She steps close.

"Enough to spend the rest of your life with me?" I wrap one arm around her, and she rests her hands on my shoulders.

"Hmmm...let me think about it. Yes."

"Good." I bend my head down and kiss her. "Because if not, that would make this a little awkward."

"Make what?"

I pull out of her arms and get down on one knee, holding up

the little box. "I have loved you since the day I met you. I waited nearly a year to tell you how I felt, and I don't want to wait anymore. Will you be my real fiancée this time around and marry me?"

Danielle brings her hands to her face and nods. "Yes! So much yes!"

I stand back up and slip the ring on her finger. "This one is real, I promise."

Danielle laughs and brings her hand to her face. "It's gorgeous!"

She's still looking at the ring as I envelop my arms around her. "Oh my God, we're actually engaged!" She makes a little squeaking noise. "For real!"

"I love you so fucking much, Danielle." I grab her ass and kiss her neck. "I can't wait until you're my wife."

"Danielle Dawson has nice alliteration. I'll sound fancy." She looks at the ring again and the sunlight sparkles off of it. "Does anyone else know?"

"Owen went with me to pick out the ring," I tell her. "But I didn't tell him when I was asking. I didn't want him to blow it."

"That was probably a good idea." Danielle's eyes get all teary as she smiles. "Let's go. I want to show this off to your family."

I take her right hand, and she holds her left hand up again, turning her fingers so the ring sparkles in the sunlight.

"Are you going to call your parents?" I ask her when we get into the car.

"Maybe not tonight, but I will." After finding out that her parents were hoping to sell the farm behind her back, Danielle confronted them. They were on the phone, and I could hear the back-and-forth yelling from the other room.

Her father thinks she's throwing her life away. Her mother seems more concerned with having to tell people her youngest daughter is a bartender. Neither were happy when Danielle told them she was staying here for good, and there were a few days there when it seemed like she'd never talk to her parents again.

And then they showed up, wanting to smooth things over. Life is too short to be angry with each other like that. You really don't know what day will be your last.

Everyone but Owen is at my parents' already. He's usually the last to arrive. Everyone is gathered in the kitchen like usual. Archer is holding Emma, and Jackson comes running to give me a hug.

"Something weird happened today," I start when Jackson goes back to his toys. That gets everyone's attention.

"Yeah," Danielle says, nodding her head. "It was really strange." She holds up her hand. "This ring just appeared on my finger."

Quinn almost drops her food. "You're serious this time?"

"Yes," Danielle and I say at the same time.

"Oh my God, congrats!" Quinn jumps up and gives us both a hug.

"Look at you!" Danielle looks down at Quinn's stomach. "You popped overnight!"

Quinn puts her hand on her baby bump. "It's part baby and part food." She gives me a hug next and then grabs Danielle's hand. She, Scarlet, and Mom gush over the ring.

"You're finally crossing over to the dark side." Dean pats my back. "I mean the married-life side."

"It's about time," Archer laughs. "I'm happy for you two."

Weston's phone rings and he steps aside to answer it. "Sheriff Dawson," he says, sounding serious.

"Remember when you and Owen called him Lord Fart Face for an entire year?" Dean asks.

I laugh. "And you were Captain Shart Pants. You got so pissed every time we called you that. So naturally we said it as often as possible."

"Because I never sharted."

"We were driving home from visiting Aunt Mary. We all smelled it for the two-hour car ride," Dad says, and we all laugh.

I look out the kitchen window, seeing Owen pull in the driveway. I'm able to sense him, as weird as that sounds. We can't really explain it, other than saying it's a twin thing. He comes into the house, already smiling. He didn't know I was asking Danielle to marry me, but he's able to sense it too.

"Glad you finally manned up," Owen says, pulling me into a hug.

"Me too," Danielle laughs, and I go back to her, wrapping her in my embrace. "Though if anything was worth waiting for, this was it."

EPILOGUE

DANIELLE

ABOUT A YEAR LATER...

"I finalized the menu for the bakery," I tell Logan, watching him put another log on the fire. He comes back to the couch, picking up the papers from the coffee table, and sits next to me.

"Are you warm enough?" he asks, reaching for another blanket.

"I'm fine," I tell him, though I know he's going to keep pampering me like crazy. He's been at it all week, and I don't think he's going to stop any time soon. "The temperature did plummet fast today."

"Yeah. But it's supposed to warm back up soon."

"I'd like that."

"Gotta love the spring weather in the Midwest. It was hot two days ago and back down to freezing today." Logan pulls my legs into his lap and starts rubbing my feet. I lean back, closing my eyes. "That feels good."

We got married in October, much to my own mother's dismay. It wasn't enough time to plan a big fancy wedding, but that's not what we wanted anyway. Just a week or so after Logan proposed, we started looking around for places to have the wedding. We joked about having our reception in an old barn, back when we were pretending to be engaged. After I had a real ring on my finger, it started to sound like what we actually wanted.

And then it just so happened that the newly restored venue in a century-old barn had a cancelation, and we were able to snag a date the first weekend in October. The weather was perfect; bright, sunny, and a crisp sixty-five degrees.

"Are you going into work tonight?" he asks, looking over the menu.

"I should if we want to make sure we're ready to open next week."

"You'll be ready." He moves his hands up my leg, and I know it won't be long until those fingers are inching toward my core. Which is fine by me. I've had the sex drive of a teenage boy lately, and Logan is very eager to please me. "Don't wear yourself out."

"I'm fine," I tell him. I just got over a nasty cold, and he's been babying me like crazy. "We're fine." I rest my hand on my stomach, hoping to feel our baby kick again. I felt her for the first time just yesterday, and I can't even describe how incredible that feeling is, and how excited I am for Logan to be able to feel her too. I'm only seventeen weeks along and am just now starting to show.

We haven't picked a name yet, but our little girl will be the fourth granddaughter in the Dawson family. Mrs. Dawson jokes that it's making up for the years when it was all boys, though now Jackson is outnumbered. He loves his baby sister dearly and is a good big brother.

"This looks good." Logan glances at the menu again before lying down with me on the couch.

"I'm nervous."

"You're going to blow everyone away."

"I hope so. At least it's already an established bakery. Fingers crossed I make it better and not worse."

"You will," he says, and I know he fully believes it. A few months ago, Mia Harris, an elderly woman who's owned a bakery on the main street in Eastwood's downtown for years, decided to put the store up for sale. It's in the building right next to the spot my grandma wanted to open her own shop.

It's a bit of a risk, but Logan and I decided to buy it. I might stick one of my pies on the counter for people to sample, but I'm more interested in the business side of it than the actual baking side. I spent the last few months coming up with a solid business plan and already have a few contracts lined up with other venues in the area.

This is the last thing I thought I'd be doing with my life. Owning a bakery. Getting married to my best friend. Deciding to start trying for a baby on our wedding night.

It wasn't easy getting to where we are. There were lots of good days and just as many bad. I made mistakes along the way. But I learned and I grew, and every time I failed, every time something didn't go as I hoped and planned, I reminded myself that I'm lucky to get to fail.

Because I'm alive, and I've made a promise to both myself and Grandpa to never take a single day of my life for granted.

Logan's lips land on mine and my heart feels so, so full. I have so much in my life to be thankful for, and I know, no matter what gets thrown at us, we'll get through it.

Together.

Owen's story is next! FIGHT DIRTY releases on June 13th, 2019.

THANK YOU

Thank you so much for taking time out of your busy life to read Cheap Trick! I had so much fun writing Logan and Danielle's story, and found writing Danielle's character to be so refreshing and cathartic, so she's a very relatable character for me.

I appreciate so much the time you took to read this book and and would love if you would consider leaving a review. I LOVE connecting with readers and the best place to do so is my fan page and Instagram! I'd love to have you!

www.facebook.com/groups/emilygoodwinbooks
www.instagram.com/authoremilygoodwin

ABOUT THE AUTHOR

Emily Goodwin is the New York Times and USA Today Best-selling author of over a dozen of romantic titles. Emily writes the kind of books she likes to read, and is a sucker for a swoon-worthy bad boy and happily ever afters.

She lives in the midwest with her husband and two daughters. When she's not writing, you can find her riding her horses, hiking, reading, or drinking wine with friends.

Emily is represented by Julie Gwinn of the Seymour Agency.

Stalk me:

www.emilygoodwinbooks.com
emily@emilygoodwinbooks.com

ALSO BY EMILY GOODWIN

First Comes Love

Then Come Marriage

Outside the Lines

Never Say Never

One Call Away

Free Fall

Stay

All I Need

Hot Mess (Luke & Lexi Book 1)

Twice Burned (Luke & Lexi Book 2)

Bad Things (Cole & Ana Book 1)

Battle Scars (Cole & Ana Book 2)

Cheat Codes (The Dawson Family Series Book 1)

End Game (The Dawson Family Series Book 2)

Side Hustle (The Dawson Family Series Book 3)

Dead of Night (Thorne Hill Series Book 1)

Dark of Night (Thorne Hill Series Book 2)

60515266R00136

Made in the USA
Middletown, DE
15 August 2019